# SILENCE IS Golden

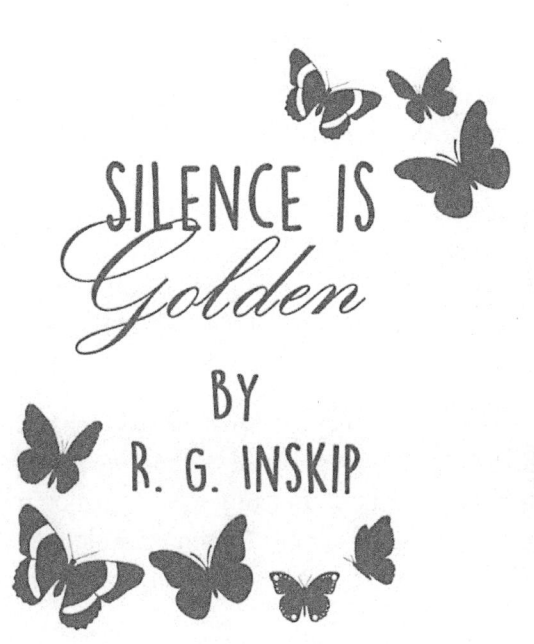

## BY
## R. G. INSKIP

Copyright R. G. Inskip 2020

This book is sold subject to the condition that it shall not, by way of trade or otherwise, be lent, resold, hired out, or otherwise circulated without the publisher's prior consent in any form of binding or cover other than that in which it published and without a similar condition including this condition being imposed on the subsequent publisher. The moral right of R. G. Inskip has been asserted.

This is a work of fiction. Any names, characters, businesses, organizations, places, events and incidents either are the product of the author's imagination or are used fictitiously. Any resemblance to any actual persons, living or dead, events or locales is entirely coincidental.

ISBN: 9798669860585

R. G. INSKIP

# SILENCE IS Golden

BY
R. G. INSKIP

**SILENCE IS GOLDEN**

# ACKNOWLEDGEMENTS

I would like to thank everyone for your continued support and encouragement. I would like to thank my family, for always believing in me, for my friends for continuing to follow my books.

For all of you, who bought these books. I hope you enjoy it as much as I enjoyed writing it.

Thank you.

SILENCE IS GOLDEN

## POEMS.

*'since I lost you, I am silence-haunted,*
*Sounds wave their little wings*
*A moment, then in weariness settle*
*On the floor that soundless swings.*

*Or Whether the people in the street*
*Like pattering ripples go by,*
*Or whether the theatre sighs and sighs,*
*With a loud hoarse sigh:*

*Or the wind shakes a ravel of light*
*over the dead-black river,*
*Or nights las echoing*
*Makes the daybreak shiver:*

*I feel the silence waiting*
*To take them all up again*
*In its vast completeness, enfolding*
*The sound of men.'*

*By*
*D.H Lawrence- 1885-1930*

SILENCE IS GOLDEN

# CONTENTS

*Acknowledgements and Dedications*

*About the Author*

| | |
|---|---|
| *Chapter 1. Isabelle* | *Pg. 1.* |
| *Chapter 2. Friends?* | *Pg.35.* |
| *Chapter 3. New Possibilities?* | *Pg.41.* |
| *Chapter 4. Party!* | *Pg.52.* |
| *Chapter 5. Sarah* | *Pg.68.* |
| *Chapter 6. The truth* | *Pg.75.* |
| *Chapter 7. Intensive Care* | *Pg.88.* |
| *Chapter 8. London* | *Pg.100.* |
| *Chapter 9. The Caravan* | *Pg.107.* |
| *Chapter 10. Smoke and Ashes* | *Pg.128.* |
| *Chapter 11. Highgate Cemetery Catacombs* | *Pg.144.* |
| *Chapter 12. I'm the Bad Guy…* | *Pg.151.* |
| *Chapter 13. Always Daddy's girl* | *Pg.172.* |
| *Chapter 14. The Close* | *Pg.180.* |
| *Four years later* | *Pg.184.* |

SILENCE IS GOLDEN

# CHAPTER 1. ISABELLE

"Isabelle are you getting up now?" Trish called from the bottom of the stairs. Isabelle tried to ignore her mother, burrowing herself deeper into the warm soft covers. "Honey?" her mother called again. Groaning, Isabelle peeled open her eyes wincing at the weak sunlight pouring in from the gap in the window. She wished she could just call down saying she'd be down in a minute, so that she could lie in her warm bed for a while longer, but Isabelle knew better than that. With a yawn she threw back the covers, she sat up, stretching her arms over her head. When the bones clicked satisfyingly, she placed them on the bed beside her. She put her feet into her cold slippers and shivering slightly she stood, going over to her vanity mirror. She frowned at her reflection then shaking her head at it, she turned away. It wasn't that she thought herself ugly, in fact she thought she was quite average, she had even been called 'pretty' a few times, with dark blonde hair that fell just past her shoulders. She had an oval face with large blue eyes a small button nose from which a small smattering of freckles sat above. She had pale skin which burnt easily in the sun. It was the scars that she hated; It was the scars that were ruining her life. She threw on her dressing gown over her nighty and sulked all the way down the stairs. It was Monday. She hated Mondays. Monday's meant she had to go to school. Her father was sitting at the table, a glass of orange juice and a large bowl of porridge with fruit in front of him. He waved at her as she entered the room. She waved back and took her seat opposite him.

"Oh good morning love, I didn't hear you come in," Trish said with a beaming smile, looks wise Isabelle was like her mother-they both had blonde hair and blue eyes, but her Mother had an elegant air about her that Isabelle lacked, she had high cheekbones like her mother but had dimpled cheeks like her father. She gave her mother a small smile, "I swear one of these days I'll just stick a bell on you, that way hear you every time you come in," joked Trish. As she turned back to the kitchen counter her father rolled his eyes at her back, giving his daughter a cheeky grin, she had to bite her lip to stop herself from giggling.

"Do you want pancakes?" Trish asked turning to look at Isabelle, who nodded eagerly "one? Two?" She asked and Isabelle held up her hand using two fingers to indicate she wanted two pancakes. "Ok, honey, two pancakes coming up," she said smiling. "Mrs. Pillar called the other day..." Trish said conversationally, "she said that her Margery's had a fall-hurt her hip poor thing-so she won't be able to help with the church meeting on

Tuesday..." she poured the pancake batter into the hot frying pan and it began to sizzle. "...so naturally she asked me to step in. I mean it's not like I haven't done it before, at least this way the tea and coffee won't taste like drain water...oh dear, that means I'll have to bake a cake...what about a red velvet cake or a good old-fashioned Victoria sponge? I'll have to call Jenny and see what kind of cake she'll be bringing...although I could try another of my carrot and cranberry cakes, they seemed to like it at the bake fair..." she mused as she flipped the pancake expertly. Trish was a baker who owned her own little catering business, she didn't have a shop but had a website that customers could use to book her for their events.

She did anything from cakes and cupcakes to hors d'oeuvre and canapés. She had already catered many weddings, birthdays, shop opening events etc. so it was no surprise that she was a dab hand in creating new and yummy treats (even if some of her experiments weren't so successful) but Isabelle had to admit that the carrot and cranberry cake was delicious. As her mother chattered away Isabelle turned to watch her father, who crossed his eyes and stuck his tongue out at her. She pulled a silly face back at him trying not to giggle. Matthew was a web designer who worked from home. He had short brown hair, with bright blue eyes and wore glasses. He had dimpled cheeks and a dimpled chin which showed up every time he gave someone one of his cheeky grins. He gave her one now and mimed 'blah, blah,

blah using the hand gesture for when someone was talking too much, mouthing the words. Instantly Isabelle snorted and giggled, she clasped her hand over her mouth then winced, clutching at her arm. Her father noticed the action and frowned at her; she hid it under the table. Trish turned around at the sound "oh honey, are you ok?" she asked concerned leaving the stove to go over to Isabelle. Isabelle nodded, trying to look reassuring "are you sure? You know you're not supposed to laugh, are you hurt?" her mother asked sending a glare at her husband knowing they had been messing around. Isabelle felt bad, she knew when she went to school her mother would have a go at her father for her own slip up. She waved her off, smiling brightly at her mother, who was rubbing her shoulder looking concerned.

Smelling something burning Isabelle pointed to the stove, "Oh *no*! The pancakes!" exclaimed Trish, she grabbed the pan off the stove and flipped it onto a cool white plate, hoping it wasn't too burned. In a way it was a good thing, Isabelle thought, it meant her mother was now distracted and would hopefully forget about her father for the time being-she hated when they argued. *'Are you ok?'* He asked her his hands forming the shapes, her father used sign language to communicate, it wasn't that he couldn't physically talk and his hearing wasn't impaired-the reason they communicated in sign language instead of just talking, it happened to dangerous if he talked, it was the same for Isabelle, she had to learn sign language at a very young age, it was also a secret. Her mother liked to fill up the silence with endless chatter, her way of coping with the...impairment, her mother knew sign language, but she liked to chatter much more than signing. Her father looked at her concerned. *"I'm fine,"* she signed back, trying to reassure him, he frowned at her concerned *"did it happen again?"* he asked feeling guilty that he'd hurt Isabelle. *"It's nothing, it's an old cut, I just caught it on the table,"* she said giving him a reassuring smile. *"Liar,"* he signed *"you're just trying to make me feel better..."* he scolded, in their house it was custom to be open and honest with each other, she smiled ruefully *"maybe..."* she signed back. *"You're going to be ok today, if those girls bother you again tell the teachers, it's what they're there for,"* her father signed to her.

She sighed-a sound she knew wouldn't hurt her, and signed *"sure,"* he gave her sympathetic look and went back to his paper as her mother placed a slightly burnt pancake in front of her, "sorry honey, I promise the next one will be perfect," she said and Izzy gave her a reassuring smile, pulling the bottle of syrup towards her, her dressing gown rode up her arm and made her scars visible. She quickly yanked the sleeve down and looked about to see if they had noticed, her father looked down at her arm and sighed, *"you don't have to hide here,"* and she shrugged *"I know... but neither do you,"* she replied looking at his high neck shirt, tie and polo jumper. He grinned and signed *"you got me there."* She picked up her knife and fork and began to tuck into her pancake, covered in syrup to mask the burn taste. "I heard that someone bought old Bennet's place, you know, across the street from us, the one that's been empty since poor Mr. Bennett died there...anyway, someone bought it, it's all been rather hush hush, but Mrs. Medley said she saw them moving in last week, they're a couple, with two sons, the eldest is set to start school today, what was his name again...Oh yes, Adrian or Aiden, something like that, but I thought maybe, you know, as he's new and all..." Trish suggested *"if you want me to be friends with him then wouldn't there have to be, you know, actual conversations?"* Izzy signed back and her mother sighed.

"Fine, be like that, I just thought it would be *nice*," she said putting another pancake on her plate, this time not burnt. "Did you hear about Mrs. Perkins from down the street? Such a terrible business..." her mother began, as she busied herself with washing the dishes. Her father rolled his eyes with a grin, and Isabelle hurriedly ate her last pancake so she could get ready for school. She dressed in her black tights, and black skirt, along with her long sleeve shirt, tie and blazer with the 'Silver Oaks High school' badge logo-a white tree in a shield with the words 'silver Oak's High school' sewn on through the middle on a scroll-on the left hand pocket the white thread standing out against the black. Slipping on her black ballet flats, she took one last look in the mirror, running her brush through her hair, trying not to look too hard in case she was her reflection again. Brushing her teeth quickly she ran down the stairs and picked up her bag slinging the strap on her shoulder. *"All ready?"* her father asked her, his fingers shaping the words effortlessly, how did he make it look so effortless? She nodded watching him smiling as he opened the door. "Wait!" her mother shouted hurrying over while wiping her hands on her apron, "where's my goodbye?" she asked, flinging her arms around her, smiling to herself Isabelle hugged her back. "Try to have a good day, today honey," she said, and Isabelle rolled her eyes, Trish sighed and kissed her forehead. "I'll come pick you up after school," she said, and Isabelle nodded. The drive to school was filled with classical music, a favourite of her fathers, it always had a way of calming her, and she rested her head against the window glass and watched as the countryside eventually gave away to the town. She liked living out in the country, it was for their own protection mostly but she liked that there weren't much people about, she could count her neighbours on her hand, and there was practically no crime here. Going back to school was like popping her idyllic little bubble and filling it with too much noise.

All too soon he pulled into the school car park. Pulling up into a parking space, Isabelle looked out of her window, to watch the other students clustered in gangs, chattering happily to each other, probably about what movies they had seen…which shops they had been to…catching up on what they had been up to over the holidays, no doubt. Seeing them talking freely, Isabelle felt a pang and looked down at her lap. That should be her, a normal teenage girl, normal social life…but that wasn't her, so she just had to get used to it, she scolded herself. Her father patted her hand, a sympathetic look on his face, she gave a small smile back to him, she hated that he thought it was all his fault. *"Not long till you're home for the weekend."* he signed making sure she saw him. *"I know,"* she signed back to him. *"See you later, have a good day at school, I love you, sweet pea."* her father signed, and she smiled at the endearment. *"Love you too dad,"* she signed, she hugged him briefly then she picked up her bag, stepping out of the car. She paused to wave at the car then faced the school. It wasn't anything spectacular about it, it was just a bunch of tall ugly red brick buildings, fenced off with an ugly green metal fence, but it was a place that filled her with a certain kind of dread.

She was supposed to start year 11 this year, her last year of school and although she was excited at the prospect that she would be leaving this place she still couldn't feel all that good about it. One of the main reasons behind this feeling was because she couldn't talk and she didn't have friends-they just didn't understand her-they thought that she was playing up, trying to get attention, but they couldn't understand the full story behind her muteness. She wasn't allowed to tell anyone, and even if she did, they definitely wouldn't believe her. Squaring her shoulders, she started walking towards the only place she felt safe. The library. It was her little safe haven, a place she could go, and no one would care if she couldn't talk, everyone was quiet here.

It was only a small library, at the back end of the school, just past the main office. Which took her by the bike shed. This was the downside of going to the library, as she would no doubt bump into Josh and his gang, who always hung around showing off about who's bike is the best, which girls would 'get it' and so on. His favourite game is tormenting anyone who was different than they were, which meant Isabelle. All too soon their loud obnoxious voices could be heard, they were laughing loudly at something one of them had said, something nasty no doubt, she thought. She walked quickly, her head down fixing her gaze on the floor in front of her, trying to look inconspicuous.

"Hey, look who's here!" Josh shouted loudly, and Isabelle cringed, ignoring him, she walked even faster. "Izzie! Wait up, what's the rush!" he shouted, "Yeah, wait up!" the others called. She pretended not to hear them but she felt a hand grab onto her arm and jerked her to a full stop. "I said wait up!" Josh said only slightly winded, he was a head taller than she was, with short cropped blonde hair, blue eyes. He was quite good looking, which he definitely knew about, with his tanned skin and straight white teeth, but Isabelle hated him, hated him with a passion. "Where are you going in such a rush? Didn't you hear me calling you?" he said she shrugged, "Yeah, are you deaf as well as dumb?" one of the others asked, she thought he was called Martin or Mitchell or something like that. The others laughed and one high fived him saying "good one!" Josh laughed with them and said "hey, the guys and I are going to hang out at the park later, wanna come? What do you *say?*" he asked trying to goad her to talk yet again, she shook her head at him, knowing the invitation was just to make fun of her, she tried to back away, but he said "God, you're so ignorant Izzie, I asked you a question? Aren't you gonna answer me?" he demanded and gritting her teeth Isabelle turned her back on them.

"You're such a bitch!" Josh said grabbing onto her wrist yet again, which surprised Isabelle so much she stumbled. He had never been this angry with her before, "take it easy, Josh," Matt said uneasily, he was ok, by their standard, but he hadn't gone out of his way to really help her. "She's not worth it," he suggested, Josh have Isabelle a contemptuous look but let go of her wrist. "Yeah, you're right," he said still scowling. Isabelle took her chance and made a run for it, picking up her pace she sped-walked the rest of the way to the library. She loved books, they were her only escape from the life that she had been dealt with, her only friends and companions. When she entered the building, the receptionist, Lynne said "good morning Isabelle," and Isabelle smiled at her. The library was just ahead of the front desk, a small room crammed with shelves upon shelves of books, the librarian Helen, smiled and waved at her. Isabelle waved back. She liked Helen, she was slightly plump, and had short light blonde hair, permed with glasses on a chain. It was quite empty this time of morning, except from a couple of older students studying, and a few nerdy boys playing computer games on the library's ancient computers. She took a seat on the table at the back, pulled out her battered copy of wuthering heights and began to read. When the bell rang, she slowly gathered her things, delaying the time when she would have to go back past Josh and his gang, hoping that they would have gone when someone shouted her name.

"Isabelle!" she turned to see Lynne the receptionist calling her, beckoning her over to the desk. Curious she walked back over to her. "There you are, I was just talking about you," she smiled "could you please show Mr. Parker to his next class, I looked at your timetable and you're both in double science together," she asked, and Isabelle looked over at the boy standing next to the desk, who was looking shy. **So, this must be the new boy her mother had talked about...**She thought, **he was kind of cute.** She blushed looking down but nodded. "Good! Well that settles it, off you two go then, oh and if you're late give Mr. Jones these," she said handing over two hall passes. They fell into step next to each other, as Isabelle kept stealing glances. He was taller than her and slim. He had dark blue eyes, with dark brown hair that was styled short at the sides and longer at the top, like a lot of boys had at the moment. He looked sideways at her and she blushed. "So...double science for first period, that sucks..." he said, smiling at her. She smiled back at him and shrugged. "So, which teachers should I avoid? Which ones would bite my head off?" he asked, and again Isabelle shrugged. "Not much of a talker then..." He joked and she pursed her lips, hadn't Lynne told him she couldn't speak? She shook her head. "Ok," he said, frowning a little. It was obvious that Lynne thought this new boy would make her talk again, or she would have just told him that she didn't talk. Not wanting to offend the newcomer, she pulled her small notebook out of her pocket with her pen and began to write:

*Sorry, I can't talk, but if you have any questions, I can write it down?*

She showed it to him, and he took the pad, reading what she wrote down for him. Understanding stole across his face then he turned to smile at her. "Sure," he said, "at least you have good handwriting," he joked, and she smiled, relieved. "So, how long have you been here?" he asked, Isabelle thought for a moment then wrote:

*All my life. I went to Sea mount primary school, then moved up here with everyone when it was time to start high school.*

He read then said "ah, so you all know each other then? Have there been many newbies? Or am I the first?" looking slightly worried. Wanting to reassure him, but not lie outright she put: *Most of us know each other from primary school, but there's been a few who've moved from other places too. They will all probably try to be friends with you at first but it'll die down.*

She promised, he nodded and grinned, "They will all want to be my friend...huh, make a change then. My old school couldn't wait to get rid of me-I'm *joking*," he said noticing the look she gave him, "but I can cope with that, it's the staring I hate, the whispering...oh well. At Least it could be worse I guess, like my father always says, I could be starving, or in poverty or something...," he joked, she really liked his smile, it was a cheeky sort of grin that made her smile along with him. She mentally shook herself, no point getting attached, the other girls will have him in their sights in no time, he was easily the best-looking guy in the whole school.

*Why did your family choose to move here?* Isabelle wrote.

"Ah, well ...we moved because of my father... he had a job offer here he couldn't refuse, rather boring really," Aiden said shrugging but clearly he was holding something back "anyway, what about you? Tell me your story," he asked Isabelle and she blushed,

*There's not much to tell!* she wrote just as evasively, smiling to herself.

He raised an eyebrow at her noticing that she too was holding things back. "I can't imagine that..." he said when she wrote nothing he shrugged. They had reached the science block, Isabelle reached for the door handle but she found a hand blocking her way, "here, let me," Aiden said, he pulled the door open so she could enter first, she was surprised that people still did that, she was under the impression that chivalry was dead. Forgetting that Aiden was not her family she used the British sign language for thank you, placing her hand flat on her chin and moving it away. "You do sign language!" Aiden said grinning then he proceeded to sign *"That's so cool,"* moving his hands naturally, like he had been using sign language for some time. She stared at Aiden with her mouth open and when she realized she snapped it shut, *"how do you know sign language?"* Isabelle asked shocked. "My little cousin is deaf, we all had to learn so we could talk to her." Aiden explained, with a pleased smile on his face, like he was happy to have surprised her with this hidden talent.

*"Well you're the only other person here, other than me, who can,"* Isabelle signed and Aiden looked at her incredulously, "what do you mean? you don't have a translator?" he asked and she shook her head. "But-how do you talk to people? Just write it all down?" Aiden spluttered indignantly, and Isabelle nodded signing *"they say because I can hear, I don't need a translator."* It was Aiden's turn to gape at Isabelle, in sudden anger. "But that's totally discrimination!" Aiden fumed his voice echoing in the corridor, *"they think I'm faking not being able to talk-"* Isabelle said *"-so they're not going to pay out money when they think that I can talk."* she shrugged. "What! But that's not fair! They shouldn't just make assumptions, if you have a valid disability then they need to accommodate for you!" Aiden shouted. A door

opened and Mr. Adams poked his head out. "What's all the shouting about?" he scolded "And why aren't you in class?" Aiden and Isabelle shared a sheepish look, "Sorry Sir, it's my fault, I'm new and Isabelle was asked to show me to our room," Aiden said apologetically, and Isabelle held up the hall pass. "And we have hall passes," Aiden added, Mr. Adams eyed them up suspiciously but said "Ok then, be off with you, go straight to class mind you or you'll both be in detention whether you're new or not!" he warned. "Yes sir, right away sir," Aiden said as Isabelle nodded frantically. As the door shut Aiden and Isabelle picked up the pace.

"Sorry about that," Aiden said and giving him a small smile Isabelle signed *"It's ok."* They walked in silence for a moment before Isabelle noticed that Aiden seemingly grappled with something. He opened his mouth but then shut it again, frowning. "S*pit it out,"* Isabelle signed, and Aiden gave her a rueful smile. "Can I ask...would it be rude if I asked why you can't talk? Is it something to do with some sort of damage or something?" Aiden asked tentatively, Isabelle thought for a moment not really sure how to word it but she began with *"It's very complicated...It's not technically medical, but it hurts me if I talk,"* she said, she expected Aiden to leave it at that but he said "how does it hurt you?" The question made Isabelle uncomfortable, and she pursed her lips. "Sorry, I'm asking too many questions again, aren't I? I'm just interested, you don't meet too many people who can't talk, I always wonder what it would be like, try to put myself in their shoes..." Aiden explained "I want to be a doctor, when I finish college," he said and Isabelle nodded *"at least you know what you want to do,"* she signed *"I have no idea,"* she shrugged. "There's still plenty of time to choose," Aiden added, she felt a twinge, whatever it was, she was sure it would have to compile to the fact that she couldn't talk, best to find a job where she could work at home, like her dad, less risk involved.

They stopped outside the science room door, *"this is us,"* Isabelle signed then she pushed open the door. Immediately all the heads in the class turned to face them and Mr. Jones stopped talking, they were only a few minutes late but he scowled all the same and said "Miss Golden you're late," looking at the clock. "That's my fault Sir, Isabelle was asked to show me to our room, we have hall passes," Aiden said as Isabelle gave Mr. Jones the passes, and Isabelle blushed-embarrassed from all the attention.

"And you are...?" Mr. Jones asked checking the register, "Aiden Parker, sir," Aiden replied and after consulting with the register Mr. Jones said "Ah yes, there you are: Mr. Parker. Well, take a seat." Isabelle rushed to the back of the room, her usual spot, keeping her eyes down to avoid catching any of her classmates. She sat and quickly took out her pencil case and her notebook, to her amazement Aiden took the seat next to her, which had always been empty until now. He smiled at her and said "can I borrow some paper? I haven't got a notebook yet..."

he asked and she nodded at him, eyes wide with surprise. She ripped out a page and mutely handed it over, wondering why the boy was still being friendly. Mr. Jones started the register, calling the names off the list. When he got to Isabelle's name, he looked up at her, not expecting any answer, but reading it out all the same. After he completed the register, Mr. Jones started up the lesson.

He was a rotund man, with balding grey hair, a stubbly beard, and glasses. He almost always wore shirts with a grey jumper. He started to drone on about refraction in a bored voice, clicking through his slideshow on the whiteboard and Isabelle dutifully began taking notes. "Err...could I borrow a pen too? Mine just ran out," Aiden whispered sheepishly, Mr. Jones looked over at them; "No talking!" he told them. Aiden grimaced an apology at Isabelle and she gave him a small smile and pulled out a pen.

As Mr. Jones droned on, Isabelle peeked a glance at Aiden, marveling that he had chosen to sit next to her, he caught her looking and grinned at her; Isabelle looked away quickly, blushing. She mentally shook herself, don't get used to it, she told herself, once he realises what a freak I am, he'll find new friends (not that they were friends) but it was the truth. She carried on taking notes, making herself concentrate and not look at the new boy. "Is he always this boring? Or is this just for my benefit?"

Aiden asked from the corner of his mouth. Isabelle grinned and wrote:

*Unfortunately, this is a normal lesson for Mr. Jones.*

Aiden picked up the paper and read it and looked up at her grinning, "at least I can talk to you-" "Can we listen to the lesson please, Mr. Parker, Miss Golden?" Mr. Jones interrupted. "Sorry, sir," Aiden apologised. Mr. Jones 'harrumphed' and carried on with his lesson, "As I was saying, **Refraction** is the bending of light as it passes from one substance to another. Here the light ray passes from air to glass and back to air. The bending is caused by the differences in density between the two substances. Therefore..." Mr. Jones continued. "Sorry," Aiden whispered to Isabelle, who smiled at him to show she wasn't angry, in fact, this was the most she had ever communicated with anyone outside of home in a very long time. Isabelle looked at the other students, most of whom were staring blankly at the whiteboard, a boy called Matt was even drooling, none of them had even bothered with her, what made Aiden different to them?

Would he too end up ignoring her the way they all did? Using her as the butt of every joke when they were bored; She hoped not, but she wouldn't get her hopes up, she could already see Stacy and the other girls giving Aiden appreciative looks, and throwing her looks of disgust and confusion. She had no doubt that after this lesson Stacy would soon pounce on him, ready to sink in her claws the first chance she got. Isabelle felt a wave of hatred wash over her. Stacy was the 'popular' girl of the school. She was the prettiest, she was the first to grow boobs, the first to wear makeup and everyone seemed to gravitate around her.

She may be pretty on the outside, but she was as shallow and as bad tempered as they came. She seemed to have a nasty Vedanta against Isabelle, not that Isabelle was much surprised at it. Stacy noticed her looking and she flipped the bird at her. Turning away quickly, Isabelle looked at the board. "What was that for?" Aiden whispered angrily, staring at Stacy, and Isabelle jumped, he had seen that? *'It's nothing...'* she signed at him, as he glared. "She flipped you off, that's not nothing!" he hissed, Stacy noticed him looking and flipped her long brown hair over her shoulder, giving him a dazzling smile, which he did not return but continued to glare, she seemed to wilt under the glare and turned befuddled to her friend, who shrugged. *'Stop that...'* Isabelle scolded *'you'll make things worse for me'* she said, "what do you mean?" Aiden asked, she was just about to answer when Mr. Jones said "Detention!"

They both jumped, not expecting him to be standing so close, "my class is for **learning**, not talking, I expect the both of you here, at the end of today," He said angrily, "but-sir, Isabelle wasn't talking, I was just-" Aiden began hotly. "Nevertheless, the both of you were still communicating-" Mr. Jones indicated to the scrap paper, which Isabelle tried to hide, knowing that it wasn't very complementary to said teacher, "I expect you both here, when school ends."

"-But sir!" Aiden interrupted "I suggest you don't finish that sentence, if you don't want another night's detention. I don't know what your last school was like Mr. Parker, but maybe next time you'll remember that in my lessons, talking is not permitted," Mr. Jones said, turning his back to them. Aiden glared after him; Isabelle stared at Aiden open mouthed. He hardly knew her and yet here he was, willing to stick up for her! She hoped her mother hadn't secretly asked him to look after her, it was the kind of thing that she would do. Aiden reached over to write on the scrap paper, he had neat handwriting, that suited him.

*Sorry, that was totally my fault,* Aiden wrote to her.

Isabelle reached over and scribbled an answer, *you didn't have to do that, you could have gotten into more trouble,* she didn't like the idea of anyone getting into trouble because of her.

*I shouldn't have been talking in lesson, rookie mistake, plus I got you into trouble, you must be mad at me, I totally understand it if you want me to leave you alone...* Aiden wrote and she shook her head at him, bending over the paper to write back: *It's not your fault, Mr. Jones is strict, I should have warned you.*

Aiden snorted, then sent a fearful look at Mr. Jones who was too busy pointing out a picture on the board to notice the noise. *So... you don't want me to go away?* Aiden asked and it was Isabelle's turn to scoff. *You're the only one here who knows sign language! Why would I want you to go away? Who would I have to talk to then?* She asked, Aiden grinned and was a little red in the face,

*Thanks, I'm glad you don't want me to go away, moving schools has been...I've been a little nervous, and you seem like a cool girl, I want to be friends- if that's ok with you? If I haven't already put you off?* He asked and Isabelle felt her face turn red.

He thought she was cool! Smiling shyly, she wrote: *I'd like that.*

Aiden grinned at her reply and they both returned to taking notes of the lesson. The bell sounded and the class started to pack up their things, "so, it says here I have math's next," Aiden said checking his timetable, "*I have English,*" Isabelle signed, self-consciously as a few students hung back, watching their interaction, "bummer!" Aiden said looking genuinely gutted, "hey, I have a brilliant idea, why don't we meet at break, then we can hang out, I hope we have some more classes together, why don't we photocopy timetables? That way it will be easier to find you, you know, if I get lost," Aiden said, he grinned down at her, beaming with his 'brilliant' idea. Isabelle found it hard to say no to him, he was like a happy little puppy, his excitement shining on his face. After giving him a shy smile, she signed 'sound's ok to me' and his smile grew even wider, "great!" he said. After a moment of smiling at each other they turned to walk out together. "So, I'm this way... I think," Aiden said squinting at the map, and pointing right of the classroom, down the large double doors at the end of the corridor, that lead to the stairs, the first English room, and the language block through another set of doors not unlike the one they were already in.

Isabelle nodded *"Just take the stairs up, take the left corridor, your room is at the end of that, Mrs. Paxton, she's alright, a little strict but overall if you keep your head down, she'll like you,"* Isabelle signed helpfully, as they reached the doors he held the door open again, impeccable manners again, "thanks, where would I be without you?" Aiden grinned, Isabelle's next lesson was at the bottom of the stairs, English with Mr. Pilsol, he was a cool teacher, with ginger hair, he liked to throw chalk at people for a laugh and never wore shoes during lessons. He also played the trumpet. *"This is me,"* she said, feeling shy again. "Right. Well...I'll see you later?"

Aiden asked hopefully, looking suddenly shy himself. *"Sure, outside the main entrance? We could go use the photocopier then,"* she replied. "Sounds like a plan," Aiden said they hesitated a second but then he said "ok, see you later," and giving a wave, turned and made his way up the stairs soon disappearing in between the hundreds of milling students, leaving Isabelle staring after him incredulously. She turned and joined the queue of students waiting for Mr. Pilsol to arrive, turning over her encounter in her head. She spent the lesson in a daze, wondering why he was so keen to be friends? After all, she was the biggest freak in this school-so why would he want to be tarred with the same brush as her?

She also worried that he would meet other people in his next lesson, cooler people than her and he would decide he wanted to hang out with them and forget about her. What if he got talking with people about her and he found out how much of a 'freak' she was to people? Locked in a battle of worry and nervousness Isabelle barely noticed that class had ended, and it took Mr. Pilsol to say her name a few times to notice she was the only one still sitting and not packing up. "Where have you been today? You look like you've got your head in the clouds," he joked and she blushed, holding up her, *"sorry,"* flash card, to which he waved it off saying, "we've all had those days, just don't let it become a habit," he grinned, and she smiled back at him as she packed up her things. The flash cards were just another, quicker way of communicating with others. She and her form tutor had made them on the computer, and laminated them so they wouldn't get ruined, it was much easier to use them in class. Now her heart gave a nervous little flutter, she was unsure as to whether or not she should go. What if he didn't show up? What if he had found someone much cooler? She didn't want to get her hopes up, she couldn't take the blow. But what if he was there and she had stood him up? A war waged inside her head as she walked. In the end reason won over her insecurities, she usually sat in the library anyway, so she might as well go and if he didn't show, she could go straight past into the library. It's no big deal, or that's what she told herself. She knew that if he didn't show she'd be gutted, she hadn't had a friend in a very long time.

She kept her head down all the way to the front entrance of the library not wanting to draw attention to herself, when she was surprised by a shout. "There you are!" Isabelle looked up to see Aiden behind her, waving. She felt herself smile as he grinned at her. Jogging to catch her up, Aiden said "you beat me." Isabelle shrugged, grinning back, as relief and happiness flooded through her. "You never said how friendly everyone is here," he said and she felt that happiness drain right back out of her, *"what do you mean?"* she asked and he said "the amount of people asking me to sit with them was unreal, it's like I'm a celebrity or something," he joked and Isabelle frowned. *"We don't get many new people moving here,"* she signed, and he laughed, the sound making butterflies flutter inside Isabelle's stomach.

"Yeah, I could tell..." he said as he fell into step beside her. *"Have you made friends with anyone yet?"* Isabelle asked timidly and he grinned "what, like besides you?" he said and she blushed, he looked thoughtful for a moment but then shrugged. "Some of the guys seem alright, I like Ollie, Kaiden, Ben and Nathan from my last class. They seem cool." he said and he caught Isabelle wrinkling her nose, "what?" he asked and she shrugged.

"Have they been not very nice to you?" he asked and Isabelle shrugged *again. "They're ok I guess, they've never been mean to me, but they have never really stuck up for me either..."* she signed, looking sad. Aiden frowned "is someone bullying you?" he asked suddenly sounding angry, "Just tell me who and I'll sort them out," he said cracking his knuckles and after noticing Isabelle looking at him with wide eyes and he said "Sorry, didn't mean to scare you, that was a joke. But seriously, if someone is being mean to you, then you need to tell someone. There's one thing I really hate and that's a bully." He had a dark, haunted look in his eyes for a moment but then it was gone, and he was watching her again, *"What happened?"* Isabelle asked and Aiden hesitated "I'd...I'd rather not talk about it," he said evasively and Isabelle let it drop, it wasn't like she could judge, she was hiding her own secrets.

Aiden opened the door for her. and they walked in silence for a bit. Isabelle tapped Aiden on the shoulder and asked *"So... did anyone ask you to hang out with them?"* she looked expectantly at him, and he said "a few actually." He had said it rather ruefully and Isabelle stopped walking; they were standing in the middle of the library now, and she turned to face him properly. *"So...why didn't you?"* she asked, afraid to hear the answer. "I told them I was meeting you," he said, and she frowned *"did anyone say anything about me?"* she asked afraid what he would say. "Err..." he hesitated, and she felt the blood rush to her face, they must have told him how much of a freak she was.

*"What did they say?"* she asked starting to get angry. "They, err, said that you tend to keep to yourself, that you, you know used to talk but you just stopped and they don't know why," he said, she could tell that he was trying to gloss over exactly what they had said. *"They told you I was a freak, didn't they?"* she said, and he frowned "no, they just said that-" he tried to explain. *"I finally get it now, they sent you to ask me why I don't talk any more, I see that now, how stupid could I be? Why would you choose to be friends with someone like me?"* she said and Aiden shook his head. "What, no, I would never do that!" he shouted *"then why are you still here after what they said about me?"* she asked angrily, *"unless someone put you up to it?"* Aiden frowned at her.

"It's because I like you, isn't that enough?" he asked, *"you don't know me!"* she signed, scowling. "Then let me get to know you!" he said, scowling right back at her, *"I know what they all think of me...and you'll be thinking just the same too. I was kidding myself thinking you'd be any different."* Her face flooded with heat and she was ashamed that tears of anger were pooling in her eyes. "Don't cry, look, I'm sorry, I feel bad that everyone has treated you this way, that they can't be bothered to get to know you, I want to be here for you, Izzy-" Aiden began and she shook her head at him. *"I don't need your pity, if that's what this is-I've done ok on my own so far,"* Isabelle signed, angry at him. "What-no! That's not what I mea-!" He shouted back, angry himself. "Sssh!" the librarian interrupted, scowling at him. He lowered his voice, "Isabelle, I want to be friends because, despite me being the new guy, you were kind to me, you didn't bombard me with questions, or judge me in any way, at least until now, you let me stay with you, when I could tell you felt uncomfortable about it, you **are** a cool person Isabelle, why can't you see that? I want to be your friend. If you'll let me. Just calm down and let's talk, please? I won't ask any questions, I promise, even if you decide to **never** tell me anything, that's fine with me, I just want to be there for you." Aiden said, "please?"

His earnest face made Isabelle calm and after a moment of silence she nodded. A relieved smile lit up his face, "thank you," he said, and she shrugged still unsure she had made the right decision. They chose a seat on a table furthest away from each other. After an awkward silence, Aiden said "I'm sorry," Isabelle looked down at her hands, pulling down her sleeves to cover her hands, not that there were any scars there, but more for the comfort of the action. "It must be very lonely. Not having anyone to talk to," Aiden said and again Isabelle shrugged. "There's no excuse for it though, there's different ways to talk to a person," he said angrily, "it sounds like there's a lot of shallow people in this school.

They're nuts not wanting to get to know you," he said. Isabelle blushed and signed *"most people tend to shun things they don't understand,"* she added a shrug at the end as if to say 'what can you do about it' and Aiden snorted. "I'm glad I'm not most people then. I hate it, the prejudice they have against someone just because they don't fit into their narrow-minded views on what's 'normal' it makes me so mad!" Isabelle saw that haunted look in his eyes again and she wanted to reach over and take his hand in hers. It wasn't that far away, it would be so easy- Aiden shook his head and said "sorry, I'm not making a good first impression, am I?" smiling ruefully at her and the moment was lost.

It seemed something terrible had happened but it had made him this person sitting in front of her. She wouldn't ask again about the look in his eyes. It wasn't her place to pry, but it gave her a feeling of curiosity which made her see herself from his point of view and it made her feel bad for shouting at him, when she herself wanted to ask him so many questions. So she just smiled and signed: *"sorry I shouted at you, and for saying you were like them."* She felt bad, after all she was acting like them by labelling him in their category when he was definitely not like the others. He smiled back at her, "It's ok." He said and they smiled at each other. A comfortable silence fell as they stared at each other. "So... what do you want to do now? Do we go copy your timetable now and go for a walk or...?" Aiden asked and Isabelle signed *"can we stay here for a bit then before the bell goes, we can go to copy our timetables? I don't like walking around out there if I can help it,"* He noticed the fear in her eyes at the thought of mingling with the other students and nodded, "sure, sounds good to me," he watched as Isabelle signed the universal sign for *"thank you,"* she smiled and he grinned back at her. "Ok so, who's your favorite author?" he asked her. It caught Isabelle off guard, who **was** her favorite author? That was such a hard question, that was like asking a parent if they had a favorite child! She narrowed her eyes at him.

*"Unfair question."* she signed crossly instead, and he laughed. "What do you mean?" he asked and she rolled her eyes. *"You can't ask someone to choose who's their favorite author! They're all so different it would be madness to pick a favorite!"* she explained "well most people **do** have favorite's," Aiden grinned. *"But I'm not most people,"* she explained *"and there's just so many books I enjoy, it would be like trying to choose who you loved the most out of your family when you love them all, but in different ways and-stop smiling at me like that!"* Aiden grinned at her, enjoying the passion he saw in her when she talked about her books. "Like what?" he asked, and she scowled *"like I'm funny, I'm not trying to be*

*funny,"* she signed, and he chuckled. "I'm just enjoying your enthusiasm." he said. She crossed her arms and glared crossly at something just to the side of him. He chuckled again then said "look, I'm sorry, so you don't have a favorite Author, that's good, I wasn't taking the mick, I promise," he said and after a while she sighed, a small smile bringing up the corner of her mouth. *"Who's your favorite author then?"* she asked and Aiden grinned. "I guess you could say I like the classics, I guess if I had to pick I would choose Hemingway," he explained and Isabelle raised her eyebrow at him, "don't knock 'em till you try them," he said shrugging and she giggled. The result was instantaneous, she gasped and winced, clutching at her arm, just below her elbow.

"Are you ok?" Aiden asked concerned half out of his chair from surprise. *"I'm Fine,"* she signed rubbing at her sore arm, "what happened," he asked looking round for whatever hurt her. *"It's ok, I just bumped my elbow on the table,"* she reassured, he narrowed his eyes at her, for she had her arms resting on the table. *"I'm fine, really,"* she continued and he frowned. "Here, let me look, maybe I can help-" he suggested and she recoiled from his reaching hand, a flash of hurt crossed his face and she felt guilty; *"it's fine, it was only a knock, it won't even bruise, I promise,"* she signed. "Ok, if you're sure..." he said still hurt; She could tell that he was still confused and suspicious but she was glad that he had chosen to drop the matter. She had to be more careful, that was twice she had let her guard down today. Too much was at stake for silly slip ups. Glancing at the clock she signed *"we better get going to the copy room, it's getting late,"* she pointed to the clock and Aiden nodded "ok," he agreed.

The copy room was right by the library, Mr. Carter was a cool, He was a young man, around his late 20's. He had a bunch of tattoos and spiky black hair. He was training to be a math's teacher, but for now was in charge of the copy room. He smiled friendly at them and gave them a copy of each of their timetables, which they exchanged. "Aw man! Looks like we only have science and P.E. together," Aiden said "bummer!" and it made Isabelle smile despite herself. At least we can have lunch together," he said. The bell rang, signaling the end of break. "Well, I guess I'll see you at lunch? Same place?" he asked hopefully and she nodded, feeling shy.

"Great! Well, see you," and they went their separate ways- Aiden off to English and Isabelle off to her R.E. room. For the rest of the day Isabelle was distracted, she kept going over the things that she had said; she kept picturing Aiden's face she liked his smile, then there was the hurt on his face when she had rejected his touch which made her feel guilty. Lunch was pretty much the same experience, they agreed to eat on a bench outside the English block, a place she pretty much avoided as it was a student hotspot, but Aiden wanted to sit out in the sun and the embarrassing truth was that Isabelle usually just ate in the empty staircase, in the drama block.

There had been a lot of staring, and whispering. She threw nervous looks around her and Aiden frowned at her, and the other students. "What's their problem?" he had asked and she wavered in telling him, but he would find out sooner rather than later, *"they don't like me, I usually keep to myself. Seeing me out here, it's confusing to them. Also, you being here with me is bound to confuse them even more."* she explained and Aiden got mad again, "they're just a bunch of hypocrites! I mean, they act all nice and friendly but they're all cowards. They see something they don't understand and they try to squash it, take a spider for example-they're useful, right? They kill bugs for us, yet we try our hardest to get rid of them, because of the way they look, and act, it's harming *us* more if we did succeed to get rid of spiders, there would be bugs everywhere. You get what I mean?" he asked and Isabelle raised an eyebrow to him.

*"Are you referring me to a spider?"* she asked grinning, and he laughed "what I'm saying is that you could-say you eventually find a cure for cancer, using spiders or something like that. Yet they still try their hardest to squash them, I'm explaining it wrong," Aiden said rubbing his hand through his hair, ruffling it up. *"I get it. Thank you,"* Isabelle signed, genuinely touched for his concern, *"it's just the way of life though, like the spider, it's in human's nature to kill something that is threatening, a DNA thing. The whole 'circle of life,' business. Nothing can change that."* Isabelle said kindly.

"But that's what I plan to change, this whole explaining it away as just a 'DNA thing' is crap. If we can change the mentality of different things with a psychologist, then it stands to reason that we can also change people's perspective of what's 'normal,' I mean, what **is** normal, am I right? If only we could make people see..." he asked, and Isabelle saw the raw hurt inside of him. He was hurting, and she wondered yet again what had caused all that hurt. He glared down at his clasped hands and she reached over placing a hand over his, making him jump and look up at her.

*"Are you ok?"* she asked kindly, and he shook his head "yeah...sorry about that, I must seem a little crazy, eh?" he asked and she squeezed his hand, *"no, not crazy. You're just very passionate,"* she said making him smile "I want to go into psychology in college, I want to be a therapist." he said "I want to help people." He glanced over his shoulder "I want to change people's views on things." he stared at a bunch of girls who had gathered to watch and whisper about them and under his glare they paled, walking away from them. *"You don't have to sit with me if they're bothering you,"* Isabelle signed guiltily knowing being with her was causing him pain.

He just shook his head and smiled sadly at her "that's exactly why I want to sit with you," he said and she frowned at him, "you don't see how cool you really are," he said and she shrugged taking a bite out of her chicken sandwich. The rest of the day was spent with a lot of staring and whispering as word spread that the 'hot new guy' was choosing to hang out with the school's biggest 'Freak'. So there she was, blushing, that at the end of her last lesson, there he was stood outside her class waiting for her. "Hey," he said in greeting, she waved her greeting, blushing at the new round of whispering, and hurried to join him. "So, that was an interesting first day, wasn't it? Hey, do you need a lift?" he asked, and she shook her head *"my dad's coming to get me, as usual, but thank you,"* she explained and his smile faltered a little, but he recovered quickly. "Cool," he said and they stood staring at each other awkwardly. "So I guess I'll see you tomorrow?" he asked hopefully, and she smiled nodding. "Good." he grinned.

She had to admit to herself, she was starting to crush hard on him, even though she hardly knew the boy. He had this aura about him most boys didn't have-yes he had a secret but so did she. She waved at him and started walking away, not sure what else there was to say. "Cya tomorrow Izzy!" He shouted, Izzy? No one except for her mother had called her that, had she just earned herself a new nickname? Had she actually made a new friend? She carried on walking, grinning to herself, making sure not to look back again. Oh what the hell, she thought as she turned her head to look over her shoulder and there he stood grinning and waving. Oh yeah, she was crushing on him hard.

# CHAPTER 2. FRIENDS?

Her father was waiting by the curb when she left the school gates, giving her a smile and a wave. For the first time in forever she smiled back and waved. Her father frowned, and as she got into the car he signed *"did you have a good day?"* and she grinned back, "yes, *it was good."* she signed back. It was far from her usual answer. Her father's eyebrows raised, he looked shocked at the answer. *"Good?"* he asked hopefully, and she shrugged. *"Something good happened today?"* he pried and Isabelle pursed her lips, thinking hard about her answer. *"I'm not sure yet, but I'll tell you if it does,"* she answered, after all, she didn't want to jinx it, or get anyone's hopes up. *"Ok,"* her father signed, but she could tell he was curious all the same.

She flicked through the radio station landing on a pop song and they drove in silence, listening to the music with her head resting on the headrest, eyes closed, a small smile on her lips. When her father opened the door Isabelle usually dumped her bag at the bottom of the stairs and slouched off to her bedroom, but instead she hung up her bag then followed her father into the kitchen.

"Oh, hello dear," her mother said in surprise, and Isabelle smiled and waved. Mrs. golden looked to her husband questioning but he only shrugged. Isabelle sat at the table, pulled over a magazine and began to flip through it absent mindedly, her mother stared at her, until she looked up and signed, *"what?"* at their confused faces.

"Nothing...you just, you usually go up to your room," her mother said with concern in her voice. *"I don't feel like hiding today,"* Isabelle signed. "Isabelle, darling, has something happened?" her mother asked, feeling a little scared at the odd behavior. *"What do you mean? I'm fine, everything's fine,"* Isabelle asked a small smile on her face. "Oh, ok then," her mother said giving her father a look. She turned back to the stove; she was making spaghetti Bolognese. The smell making Isabelle's mouth water. "Did you have a nice day at school?" her mother asked casually, but sneaking a glance at her out of the corner of her eye, she was still trying to find out the reason for her cheerful behavior, instead Isabelle just shrugged.

She didn't want to get any of their hopes up. Her mother wanted her to have friends, be a normal girl, despite her condition, but the last time she had had friends, it hadn't turned out so well... she didn't want to get hurt, or her parents to be hurt, or worried about her. "Mrs. turner said that the new boy, what was his name, Adam? Andrew? Anyway, she said he started school today," she said conversationally, with the sneaking glances. Isabelle couldn't help but smile and shake her head, her mother was so predictable, and a huge gossip too. "Have you met him yet? Mrs. turner said that he's a lovely boy, very polite..." she asked and Isabelle shrugged, "I hope the other children were nice to him. It's not easy being new you know, moving to a new area. I can imagine it being very scary," her mother said and again, was answered with a shrug.

It was Isabelle's move if she didn't know how to answer something, and her mother was on to her and would most likely not let this drop until she knew what was wrong. It was one of the reasons that her parents got together, she was like a dog with a bone and whatever she wanted with a lot of persistence she ended up getting her own way eventually.

Letting it go for now her mother started dishing up dinner, it was nice to not have to call Isabelle downstairs for her dinner, instead she was here, which was a nice surprise, but she suspected outside influence. Isabelle signed thank you, her hand on her chin, bringing it down and back up again then she began to tuck into her 'spag bol'. Her mother shared another knowing look with her father and they smiled at each other. It was nice and annoying to Isabelle that her parents could communicate with just a look, like their thoughts were in sync.

They were half way through the meal, listening to her mother chatter away, when Isabelle's phone did something it had never done before, it dinged, signaling a new message. The innocent sounding noise seemed to echo and all heads turned to her bag which hung up in the hallway. "I wonder who that could be?" her mother asked "well, aren't you going to get that?" Isabelle looked at her with round eyes, he did *not* just text her, did he? She lurched up clumsily and hurried off to fetch her phone. Once she got it out of her bag, she checked the screen. It was Aiden.

'HEY WHAT'S UP? THOUGHT I'D CHECK UP ON YOU. DO YOU WANT A LIFT TO SCHOOL TOMOROW? IT WONT B ANY TROUBLE. I ASKED MY DAD AND HE ALREADY SAID YES.'

He had even sent one of those smiley face emojis, the one that looked goofy, with its tongue sticking out. A grin cracked over her face and she had to fight down the urge to giggle, he was such a good person. "Who is it?" her mother asked and Isabelle hesitated, did she tell her? She didn't want her parents worrying about her but she could tell she had them spooked, they already knew something was up and they could jump to conclusions and think that she was going off the rails again. She couldn't just pass this one off as an accidental text from someone.

*"Its Aiden, the new boy, from across the road,"* she began, and her father frowned, her mother squealed. "I *told* you you'd make friends, Mrs. Turner said he was a lovely boy, and she's never wrong!" her mother gushed. Isabelle made a slowdown motion and signed *"we're not friends, at least not yet, he's new and I was asked to show him*

*around, he'll probably make new friends when he's settled in,"* she was not about to get any one's hope's up let alone her own. Still...the text was a step, the only other people who sent her texts were her mum and dad, but that didn't count. They had to like her they were her parents. "Oh, please! He likes you, if he didn't he wouldn't have texted you," her mother waved her off, Isabelle frowned at her, this was a bad idea. Her mother was getting her hopes up already. "So... what did he say?" Her mother asked, *"just a question about a science project,"* she lied. She didn't want to encourage her, and telling her that he wanted to give her a lift to school would probably give her a heart attack.

"Oh, that's...nice," she said sounding unconvinced, and Isabelle thought it best to get out of there. Picking up her empty plate she rinsed it and put it into the dishwasher. *"Going upstairs, homework..."* Isabelle signed, and before her mother could say anything else, she turned and practically ran up the stairs. Isabelle sent a quick reply to Aiden:

Isabelle: SORRY, I CAN'T. DAD LIKES TO TAKE ME TO SCHOOL, IT'S HIS THING. BUT THANK YOU ANYWAY FOR THE OFFER.

She added a smiley face, and pressed send. Her heart thumping in her chest. Her phone pinged and she opened the message smiling.

Aiden: K, NO PROBLEM, MAYBE NEXT TIME THEN. SEE YOU AT SCHOOL? SAME TIME SAME PLACE? He asked, adding a grinning emoji face at the end.

Isabelle: YES. OK, SEE YOU THERE!

She sent quickly, sending a smiley face back at him. He replied with a few goofy emoji faces, which made Isabelle giggle. That night she didn't sleep all that well. Lying awake she had all these thoughts running through her head, and although she felt optimistic about Aiden Isabelle was still scared of getting hurt again.

# CHAPTER 3. NEW POSSIBILITIES

The next few weeks went by in a blur of school and Aiden. They texted every evening, but she refused to 'car share' with him. She couldn't get her mother's hopes up, no matter how much she found herself getting her own hopes up. Being friends with him brought both the good and the bad; on the one hand she found herself enjoying his company more and more. They talked and goofed around, he had made it his mission to try to make her laugh and despite the danger of her condition she found she very much wanted to laugh and joke right back with him. It was a dangerous line to walk on but she found she could manage it ok if she concentrated. Isabelle woke every morning with a new kind of excitement. *She had a friend!* She bounced out of bed, with a spring in her step. She smiled at her parents as she entered the kitchen, gaining a confused smile from her mother.

"Good morning love, did you sleep well?" she said, and Isabelle gave her an enthusiastic nod. She ate a breakfast of pancakes, then went to get changed. Then the doorbell rang. She froze, one shoe still in her hand, *who would be ringing at this time?* She thought. Curious she walked down the stairs, to find both her parents looking confused. They opened the door to find a very sheepish Aiden. He stood there, an apologetic look on his face. "Hey, Mr. and Mrs. Golden is, err, is Izabelle in?" he asked nervously. They stepped aside so he could see her and she stared open mouthed at him. "Hey, Izzy," he said, giving her a shy smile, and she glared at him. *"What are you doing here?"* she demanded, face flaming red, and he bit his lip.

"You know when I said you could have a lift yesterday?" he asked, his own face a light shade of pink. Isabelle shot a look to her parents who were watching them and then she nodded begrudgingly. Aiden fidgeted, and scratched the back of his neck, "only...this is gonna sound pretty forward but you don't think I could maybe catch a lift with you? My dad's car broke down last night and well there's no bus stops close to the school so I just thought that we could go together...I mean, I'll understand if it's not ok...I just-I can walk if it's gonna be a problem..." he said, and Isabelle's mother grinned widely, before she schooled her face into an appropriate concerned look.

"Oh no! I hope your dad gets it fixed. It will be no problem at all for you to ride to school with Isabelle today, will it honey?" Isabelle's mother said, looking at her husband who frowned at the boy in front of him. He nodded. "You can have a lift any time you need," her mother said and her father raised an eyebrow at her. He looked the boy up and down, sizing him up. "Thank you, Mrs. Golden. It'll only be until my dad gets the car fixed," Aiden said gratefully. "Oh, please, call me Trish. Anything for a friend of my daughter," she said with a chuckle, and Isabelle rolled her eyes and grabbed her bag. She took Aiden's upper arm to drag him away from her mother before she said anything else embarrassing, "Nice to meet you, Mrs. Golden!" he called over his shoulder. "Have a good day you two!" she called back. Isabelle didn't know how to feel, she felt both angry and flattered; She didn't know how he knew where she lived! Why he didn't just text her instead of turning up at her door like that? Still, she was glad he had thought of her first before anyone else in the school.

She opened the back door of the car and gestured for him to go in. She got into the other side, behind the driver seat and turned to face him as her father pulled off the drive. "I'm sorry," he said, feeling awkward about having to ask for help. *"How do you know where I live?"* she asked and he gave her a rueful smile. "A woman came to the door, Mrs. medley, I think she said her name was...anyway she bought cake and gave my mum the low down on everyone on the street." he said with a chuckle, "I think my mum enjoyed the gossip," Isabelle smiled despite herself, and signed *"Mrs. Medley is the biggest gossip there is,"* she could bet that she was already gossiping to all the others on the street about Aiden's family already. Aiden sent a look up to her father who was watching them every now and again in the rear-view mirror. "Thank you for this, Mr. Golden, I can give you some money for the petrol if you-" Isabelle tapped him on the shoulder as her father waved him away, *"my father's like me, he can't talk either, only ASL."* she signed "he's the one who taught me sign language," Aiden looking flustered said "Oh, I'm sorry, I didn't know..." looking apologetically from Isabelle to her dad. They lapsed into silence for a while, both sharing glances when suddenly he broke out into a grin which made Isabelle smile back, "awkward?" he asked and she bit back a giggle, nodding. "I really *do* appreciate this," he said, and she shrugged it off, to say it was fine. Pulling into the school parking lot, her father turned around in his seat. He looked at Aiden curiously, and signed: *"who taught you to sign?"*

Aiden looked to Isabelle and back again, saying "My twin sister was deaf." he seemed to apologize to Isabelle with his eyes-wait, he said his cousin was deaf, he had a twin? Where was she? Isabelle thought. *"Was...?"* her father asked, and Aiden fidgeted again looking to the floor and said, "she died." and Isabelle's stomach dropped, why hadn't he told her before? Why was she only finding out now? Why had he lied? *"I'm sorry to hear that..."* her father signed, "it's ok. I just don't like to talk about it." Aiden said and her father nodded, *"you two better get off to school,"* he signed, and both teens nodded. They got out of the car, and after waving goodbye, they fell into step beside each other. Aiden broke the silence first, "I'm sorry I lied, you've got to understand, it was a very hard time for us. I really don't like talking about it if I can help it," and Isabelle looked up at his hurt face, this was the reason for those haunted looks in his eyes, his twin had died. *"I understand. I'm sorry about your sister..."* she signed and he gave her a sad smile. "It's the reason we moved over here, a new start, for all of us." without realizing what she was doing she reached over and took his hand, squeezing it to show him she was there for him. She could see at first that he was surprised but then he wound his hand through hers, interlocking their fingers. "Thanks." he said. She wouldn't ask anything about it-it wasn't her place to pry, he would tell her when he was ready. She was glad he had decided to tell the truth, if eventually. Plus it wasn't like she didn't have her own secrets. They parted to go to class, and as she watched him go, she thought that he was very brave.

\*\*\*\*

Aiden practically bounced up to her, at their usual meeting place, with a huge a smile on his face. *"You look happy,"* Isabelle signed and he shrugged "It's a nice day, do you mind if we eat by the picnic benches?" He asked, taking her by surprise. *"Why?"* she asked he knew she hated being around people, he only smiled wider, "Ben, and the gang invited me to eat with them, he said to bring you," and Isabelle shook her head, oh no way was that going to happen, Aiden's face fell, "you...don't want to?" he asked and she shrugged *"you know how I feel about crowds,"* she signed and he sighed. "Ok, fine. I'll just tell them another time, then," he said, Isabelle looked at his face, she could tell that he really wanted to go, she steeled herself and then said *"you should go,"* when he raised a brow at her she said *"I won't stand in the way of you making friends,"* she didn't want him to leave her but it was selfish of her to think he would want to spend all of his time with her, after all they were just friends. That's all they could be. "No, it's fine, honest. I'm eating with you." he said, beginning to walk to their usual eating area, she pulled on his arm, shaking her head.

*"No, go, there might not be another time."* she signed, persistent, "if you think I'm gonna leave you to eat alone, you're crazy." he said, and she sighed. *"I'll be fine!"* she insisted, and he clenched his jaw, "No. I'm not going without you," he said, were they having their first fight? She wondered, frustrated she shook her head. There was only one option for them. She wouldn't want him to resent her as a friend. And he would resent her for not letting him make other friends. She took his arm and started to stomp over to the benches. "Where are we going?" he asked a grin spreading across his face. She pointed to the back of the science block, towards where the benches were. "They'll be so happy to see us," he said and she rolled her eyes, they would be happy to see **him**. They thought she was a freak. This was going to suck, bad. When they came in sight of the other's, Ollie stood

and shouted, waving them over. Once Aiden got to the benches, the guys clapped him on the shoulder, "good to see you, man," Ollie said, "you've finally decided to join us," another said, she couldn't quite recall his name, he had bright red hair, was very tall and skinny, "let's face it, you missed me, didn't you?" he slung an arm around Aiden's shoulders and joked with him and they laughed together, it was nice to see.

"I had a hard time convincing this one it was a good idea," Aiden said, reaching out to ruffle Isabelle's hair, she glared at him. "Err...hey, Izzy, you doing ok?" Ollie said a little embarrassed, he looked even a little guilty, she nodded at him, and he smiled "good..." he said. "Ok, scootch up, everyone, make some space," The red head said, the rest of the guys shuffled around and Isabelle found herself sitting next to Aiden and the redhead. Ollie had opted to lounge on the floor with an Emo looking guy, while a blonde, and two brunettes sat opposite. "I think introductions are in order, I'm Ben," he said and sudden recognition flooded through Isabelle, he must have dyed his hair and grown at least a foot since they last saw each other, his natural hair was a light brown.

"That's Kaiden," he pointed to the blonde, he was small and skinny, with a round-ish face, "Nathan," he pointed to the first brunette, he was good looking enough, but not as good looking as Aiden was (Aiden was model material in Isabelle's eyes, with his pouty lips, strong jawline and bright blue eyes) Ben gestured to the other brunette, who's hair was longer than the others, it was stick straight and tied back in a man bun, "this is Liam," Liam smiled friendly, and said a small "Hey," he looked a bit like a Viking from the History channel series with that hairstyle, which was probably what he was going for.

"You obviously know Ollie and that dick head over there is Kyle," he grinned at the Emo boy, who flipped him off. "This everyone, is Isabelle," Ben said with a flourish, "we know who she is, you noob," Kyle said shaking his head "yeah, but we haven't really talked before that much, have we?" he asked then gasped and covered his mouth, blushing hard he said "sorry." He said realizing he had said 'talked.' It was hard to be mad at him, he was funny, and dramatic so Isabelle just smiled and shrugged, signing pointedly to Aiden to translate for her. "She says it's ok," Aiden said understanding fluid movements of her hands as she used ASL, Aiden grinned and said "and yeah, no problem."

Isabelle thought for a moment about what it was she wanted to say then signed *"Tell them, they don't have to dance around it, it's ok if they mention 'talking' around me, it doesn't bother me,"* Isabelle signed and others stared between them, "she says that it's ok to mention talking around her, she won't be offended," Aiden elaborated. They were quiet for a moment, taking it all in, before Ben shouted "Dude, you know sign language? That's so cool!" he said and Aiden shrugged, "my sister was deaf." he said, opting for the truth this time around.

"Was?" Ollie asked sympathetically and Aiden nodded "she ugh...died." he shifted uncomfortably, and they all gave him sympathetic looks, "aw, man, I'm sorry." Ollie said patting his back and Aiden shrugged.

After an awkward silence, Ben sighed and said "at least Isabelle's got you now, it must suck not being able to talk..." he said and Isabelle shrugged again she signed *"it's much better now I can sign with you, I'm not as...lonely,"* she told Aiden and he smiled a shy smile at her. "What'd she say?" Liam asked and Aiden explained "she says she's not lonely any more now she can talk to me," and the others looked guilty "yeah, look Izzy," Ollie began, using Aiden's nickname for her "I'm sorry, we haven't really, you know, gotten to know you, an' all that, and with what happened before...I'm sorry," Ollie looked sheepish.

Isabelle couldn't really blame him for not sticking up for her when the 'popular' kids bullied her, it was a hard world out there and he could have found himself on the receiving end if he had tried, but it was still hard knowing he had watched her tormentors and turned away. She just gave him a shy smile back, not really knowing what to say. The others nodded and murmured in agreement, Aiden looked at Isabelle to see her reaction, it was clear that he had spoken with them about her. She thought for a moment then signed *"you talked with them about me, didn't you?"* she asked, and he shrugged looking rueful. "Maybe," he said and she sighed. She didn't need a knight in shining armor, he was trying too hard to make people like her. She shook her head at him. Ben wanting to end this awkward silence let out a loud burp, and the guys erupted in noises of disgust. "Aw man that stinks!" Nathan shouted, "what did you *eat* last night?!" he said, wafting his hand in front of his face, "what?!" Ben said defensively, "I only had a *mild* curry," he said, and they snorted and said. "Just don't let it come out of the other end!" Nathan said and he chuckled. "Well, I'm not apologizing, you know how much I like my curries!" Ben said and they laughed.

They started chatting and eating, Isabelle was just content to listen to them. It was clear that Ben was the joker of the group, but Nathan was just as funny. Kaiden was the shy one, whereas Ollie and Liam were the more 'grown up' of the group and then there was Kyle. He was the gloomy, sarcastic one. She supposed that Aiden was more like Ollie and Liam, but he had much more going for him personality wise. She found herself surprised when the bell went, that she had quite enjoyed herself. They packed up continuing to take the mick out of Ben. "See you later, man?" Aiden said and Ollie clapped him on the shoulder "see you later," he said them turned to Isabelle "it was good meeting you, see you around?" he made it like a question, he still was uncomfortable around her, she just smiled and shrugged. The others called goodbyes and waved. Then it was just the two of them, "see, that wasn't so bad was it?" he asked her, bumping his shoulder into hers. She shrugged as an answer but he wanted to know exactly what she was feeling so he stopped her, "did you have a bad time?" he asked concerned he didn't want to upset her in any way. "*I don't think Ollie liked me being there,*" she signed, and Aiden shook his head "he just feels bad about how he treated you in the past. He feels guilty," Aiden said, and Isabelle nodded, she had gathered that much herself. "Do you think you'd sit with them again? Tomorrow maybe?" he asked hopefully, and she thought for a moment, she was content just to eat alone, but if it meant that much to him, she nodded. The grin that split his face then was worth the nerves and the insecurities though.

## CHAPTER 4. PARTY?

The next month flew by rather quickly. It was full of Aiden, the other guys and school work. They always texted each other every evening before bed, which was as surprising as it was endearing. He always ended his texts with one little X. It probably meant nothing, most people ended their texts with a kiss, but it made Isabelle's heart flutter. She was getting herself in deep waters, she was beginning to fall for him, which was dangerous. If he knew about why her family can't talk...she didn't know what he would do. She continued to eat at the benches with the guys, Ben was becoming her favorite, she was still a little distant with Ollie but they had all integrated her into the little group, something that was a little strange for Isabelle. It had been such a long time since she had anything close to friends.

Aiden knocked on her front door, and she rushed to greet him, his father's car was fixed now, but it had become routine for Aiden to get a lift with her into school. Her mother was happy for her, but her father was still concerned, though he tried to keep it from her. She knew him, and she knew he was unhappy about the 'new boy' showing interest in his little girl. He grinned as soon as the door opened, and said "hey, princess," it was how he greeted her now, she didn't know why, but he tried it out once and it stuck. She grinned and signed *"hello,"* he looked over her shoulder to shout "good morning Mrs. Golden!" and her mother shouted back "Good morning Aiden," she loved that he was respectful of the older generations, "what are you making today?" he asked as she came up to them wiping her hands on a cloth. "Peanut butter cookies," she said and Aiden said "sounds delicious!" his stomach growled "are you hungry?" she asked laughing and he gave her a rueful grin. "Mum's insisting on 'eating healthy' we've only got fruit or those weird healthy breakfast cereals in-I'm not a huge fan..." he said with a mock shudder and Trish giggled.

"Oh, well, that won't do at all will it? wait here and I'll go get you some of those cookies," she went off to fetch him some. "Your mother is Awesome!" he sighed and Isabelle giggled. She slapped a hand on her wrist, making a quiet hissing sound. "Hey, you ok?" he asked she had obviously hurt herself, she nodded her head, pulling her jumper further down her hand. "You sure?" he asked again, and she forced herself to smile and nod. "You know, that's the first time I heard you giggle," he commented "you should do it more often, it was cute," he said and she stuck her tongue out at him. Her mother came bustling back with the cookies as her father made his way downstairs, he was dressed as usual in a polo neck jumper, and jeans. "Hey Mr. Golden," Aiden said in greeting and her father waved. "Right you two, have a good day at school, and don't get into too much trouble," her mother joked. Aiden grinned, and said "no worries there Mrs. G." He got on so well with her mother and Isabelle found herself smiling at him, her father caught the look and raised a brow at her. She looked away quickly, she didn't want her father to know just how much she liked him. She was afraid he would tell her to stop being his friend. Not seeing their small interaction her mother kissed her on the cheek. "See you later, honey," she said, and Isabelle waved goodbye. They sat in the back of the car together, as usual, chatting about classes, and the teachers. All the while her father kept stealing glances at them from the mirror. She knew that they would talk about this later. She hoped he would understand.

They walked to the benches to talk to the 'gang' before school started, and they were greeted in the usual, happy way. Ben had taken a liking to Isabelle and whenever he saw her he would shout her name out very loudly and run to give her a huge bone crushing hug which would cause Isabelle's cheeks to flame with embarrassment. But it was just in his nature, he was a touchy feely type of guy. Sure enough, this morning was no exception. After he pulled out of the hug, he threw an arm around Aiden and said "hey, man!" giving him a manly sort of shoulder shake. The others waved and said 'hey'. "So...great news everyone! The 'rental's have informed me that this weekend, I'll have the place entirely to myself," he boasted and the guys eyes lit up, "everyone up for a party?" he asked and Nathan rubbed his hands together, "Wicked!" he said and the others seemed to be really excited too, "nice one!" Liam said, giving him a high five. "You think you can get us some booze?" Liam asked and Ben winked, "already got it sorted mate!" he whispered conspiritally. "Any hot girls coming?" Nathan asked and Ben tapped his nose, "gonna invite some more people today, but there's definitely gonna be some hot girls there," he said and they grinned and laughed.

Ben turned and looked to Aiden and Isabelle, "you two are coming, right?" he asked hopefully, and Aiden hesitated "err...I'm not sure." he looked over to Isabelle. "Aw! Come on man! It'll be mint!" Ben whined "yeah, it'll be fun!" Liam said and even Kaiden nodded, "yeah," they agreed. He sighed and said, "What do you think?" to Isabelle, she signed *"you can go if you want to, I won't stop you,"* she didn't want him missing out on anything. "Maybe next time..." he said instead, and their faces fell, "well...what about you, Izzy?" Ben asked hopefully, and she hesitated, Aiden answered for her "it's not really her kind of scene," and she smiled apologetically. "Aww..." Ben whined, pouting, cottoning on to the real reason Aiden was saying no. Nathan said "man, you're so whipped! You need to open your wings once in a while, do some solo flying, am I right guys," the lads looked at Aiden with a knowing grin and Aiden blushed. "Shut it," he mumbled to him, giving Nathan a playful shove. "I'll have to see if my *parents* haven't planned anything first. Ok?" Aiden said and they nodded begrudgingly.

"Well...just consider it, yeah? Both of you?" Ben asked looking from one to the other. "It's at 7:00, on Saturday, if you change your minds and *do* want to come...here you go, take one of these," he handed over a piece of paper with his hand written address on. "Thanks," Aiden said, taking it. "No worries," Ben replied as the bell rang signaling the end of lunch.

As they went over to class, Aiden stuffed the piece of paper in his trouser pocket, and Isabelle gave him a sideways glance. She bumped her shoulder into his, and he said "what?" with an air of nonchalance. Isabelle gestured with her head to the others as they walked towards the textiles room, she signed *"why did you say no to the party?"* she asked him and he sighed, raking a hand through his hair. "I knew you'd say no, and I don't feel like going on my own," he said, and she shook her head at him.

*"We don't have to be joined at the hip; you can go have fun without me. I'm not stopping you, so you shouldn't feel guilty,"* she felt a little flattered but she didn't want to be in the way of him having fun. "It wouldn't be fun without you," he said and she sighed *"do you want to go?"* she asked and he shrugged, she could tell he did want to, she knew she was about to be railroaded into another uncomfortable situation. *"If I went to the party, you would go too...?"* she asked, and he contemplated. "If you **wanted** to go, then yeah, I'd go too," he said but with a small smile. *"Then we'll both go,"* she signed

begrudgingly and he full out grinned, both of his dimples popping out in his cheeks, making Isabelle's heart flutter. "You're not just saying that to make me go are you?" he asked and she raised a brow at him, "I don't want you to go if you don't want to," he told her and she smiled, *"I want to go,"* she lied slightly, the truth was, the idea of a party frightened her, but it was worth it to see his grin. "Then it's a date!" he said, and she felt her face flame, it probably was just a figure of speech but it made her nervous.

"See you at lunch?" he asked, stopping outside her door, he was just down the corridor from her, in the higher up set of ICTs. She nodded and waved as he walked off to class, as she watched him go her smile slipped, she was going to regret agreeing to the party, no way her parents would let her go. She would have to make up a different excuse. Ollie and Kenzie were in her next class, Citizenship, and they nodded and smiled at her in greeting as she went over to their table. Mrs. Shenton was there already, shuffling papers sitting at her desk. She was very pretty, with her dyed blonde hair, around late 30's, so most of the guys had little crushes on her. She looked a bit like that actress who played Ronnie in EastEnders, Samantha Womack. When she started talking most of the boy's class sat up alert, listening intently or else ogling her. Isabelle shook her head at them and started taking notes. The lesson was the same as usual, homework was set, and they were dismissed. As she gathered up her things, she heard some of the girls giggling, Stacy came over to her, looking back to her friends and snickering. "Oh, hey, Isabelle, there's a party tonight, you want to come?" She asked, "what do you **say**?" she asked then all her friends laughed. "Oh wait, I forgot! You can't say anything, can you, aww, shame." she mocked, and Isabelle felt embarrassed tears fill her eyes, her face burning. "Leave her alone, Stacy," Ollie said, and she gave him the skank eye. "Excuse me?" she demanded, hand on her hip. "I said leave her alone," he repeated, coming to stand with Isabelle, "I heard what you said. It's just that...why do *you* care all of a sudden?" she asked, flipping a strand of her brown hair out of her face, she was a 'popular' girl, maybe the whole leader of the popular girls, no one stood up to her. Ever.

"Well I could ask you the same thing, Stacy. Why are *you* being such a bitch?" he asked and a few of the people who had stopped to watch said "**ooh burn**!" and it was Stacy's turn to blush. "Whatever!" she said snottily "like I care what you think, **dork**!" Ollie glared at her, and taking Isabelle's elbow he said, "Come on, Izzy, before the nastiness catches," he pulled her along, until they got to the corridor, Isabelle looking at him wide eyed. "Sorry about that," he said, still looking mad. She gave him a questioning look and he said, "people like her, they're never happy till they make someone else unhappy," he said and she nodded. "An-well, think of this as me trying to make up for all those times I didn't stick up for you," he said. "You must have been so lonely and I wasn't particularly nice to you. So, yeah...Sorry." he finished and she felt her eyes fill up again, this time with gratitude. Surprising them both she reached over and gave him a huge hug. He awkwardly patted her back and said, "it's ok," understanding her thank you and she pulled away, wondering what on earth had possessed her to do that? Aiden called out to them, waving, and after giving each other an awkward smile they hurried over.

\*\*\*\*

Isabelle's stomach was in knots. She felt so nervous, she told her parents that they were only going to the cinema but she knew that if they found out the truth that they would blow a gasket. She was also terrified that she was going to a party, especially after what happened last time. It was a mistake! She would have to call Aiden to tell him she had changed her mind. The doorbell rang which made her jump, her heart racing, and her mouth dry. Too late! She took one last look in the mirror and took a steadying breath. She had dressed in a light grey jumper and her skinny jeans with pumps; she hadn't gone overboard with her make up either, choosing to use a little bit of mascara and lip balm. Probably too casual for a party but she had to cover all of her skin-plus wearing too much make up would make her mother suspicious. It did look perfect for a cinema trip though, which would help with the plan. Aiden was picking her up, she could already hear him chatting with her mother. He would then walk with her down to Ben's house which was a couple of streets away. She grabbed her handbag, stuffing her phone in her pocket and went downstairs. Aiden turned to face her when she got halfway and he grinned up at her. He was giving her his megawatt smile that took her breath away; he really was so handsome. Especially dressed in his black top, dark jeans and grey hoodie. They even matched a little, she was glad she had chosen her own outfit. He said "hey, Izzy!" and she smiled right back, feeling less nervous now that he was here. She waved her hello, and her mother smiled at them both, "well, you two have a good time, stay safe and ring me if you want picking up," Trish said, and Isabelle nodded while Aiden grinned saying "no problem, Mrs. G." Using the new nick name he had started calling her mother which made her mother giggle like a school girl!

It was slightly cool outside but not cold. The slight breeze lifted Isabelle's hair as she walked, and she shivered. Sure, she wore a jumper but she still felt chilled. Aiden saw and said, "Do you want to go back to get a coat?" It was cute that he was concerned but if she were to go back in, she would have definitely changed her mind. She shook her head and he shrugged. They walked in silence for a bit, and it was a little awkward, but she guessed that was because this would be the first time they socialized outside of school. Aiden sighed and pushed his hands deeper into his pockets, "starting to get colder now, I miss the sun already," he said conversationally, and Isabelle nodded. *"Was it warm then, where you're from?"* she asked she hadn't asked him too much about where he had come from and despite her concern that he would shut down or be mad at her, he just laughed.

"Pretty much the same as here, I'm from Manchester." he said and she grinned sheepishly. So not that far from here then; she felt a little stupid. *"This must all seem pretty slow to you, compared to Manchester."* she signed, and he shrugged, "It's not too different. It's just a bit smaller and a bit greener in places here..." he said, and she nodded. "I was just saying that I miss the sun, I'm not too great with the cold. My family goes abroad in winter a lot." he explained and she grinned *"I've never really been abroad, me and my dad...can't go, it's...hard to explain to people about us,"* she signed her smile slipping, *"I wish we could go though, the way people talk about their holidays."* she looked a little wistful. "When we finish school, I'll take you, we will have a great time, you'll see," he said and she just smiled sadly, *"maybe,"* she just signed. She would not get her hopes up.

They had arrived outside of Ben's house, music was pumping and there were people already drunk, lounging on the grass, one waved and said "Hey, whassup!" slurring, Aiden nodded his head at the boy and said "Alright?" they walked by him. *"I'm thinking this was a bad idea,"* Isabelle signed and Aiden chuckled at her, "it's just a normal party, there's bound to be alcohol," he said and she frowned, he didn't expect her to drink did he? She couldn't, she had promised her parents never again. He grasped her hand, saying "when it gets too rowdy, we'll go home," he promised, leading her through the hall. She stared at her hand, clasped in Aiden's, and she got butterflies. He was holding her hand! They walked down the hallway, past couples making out, to the kitchen.

Ben wasn't here, but by the looks of it, this was the 'bar' with the counters littered with bottles of alcohol, empty plastic cups, bags of crisps, chocolates, there were half eaten boxes of pizza and peanuts. Aiden leaned down and shouted over the music "do you want some pop?" and she nodded, he grabbed two cans of Pepsi, and gave one to her. "Wanna go find Ben?" he asked, and she nodded, knowing he was anxious to show him they had arrived. The living room had been made into a makeshift dance floor; the furniture pushed back to the walls. There wasn't a DJ or anything like that, they had simply put you tube on the TV and were taking it in turns to choose music. Not that a DJ would have fitted in his cramped living room. Isabelle's heart was racing, she had been to parties, a very long time ago, and it wasn't a memory that she wanted to revisit. Aiden spotted Ben and the guys over the heads of the other party goers and he pulled Isabelle through till they stood in front of them.

"Hey man! You made it!" Ben shouted, throwing an arm around Aiden's shoulders, sloshing his drink in the process. "Careful, he's *very* drunk." Ollie warned, and Aiden de-tangled himself, Ben tried to make his eyes focus and he eventually grinned and said "Oh, hey Izzy!" shouting a little too loudly, she waved at him, smiling fondly. "I think that this party is going to start getting out of hand, is there anything that his parents don't want broken?" Aiden said looking around, "already taken care of," Liam said looking tipsy himself. "Does Ben even know half these people here?" Aiden asked Ollie and he shrugged. "You know Ben, he'd invite the whole school, if he could fit them in here," he said, and Aiden chuckled. Looking at how all the other girls were dressed Isabelle couldn't help but feel very under dressed, with their short skirts and dresses. Isabelle zoned out while Aiden talked with the guys, and she started to look around. Kaiden was looking around too but seeming shy; he looked a little out of place here, but then again so was she. She gave him a small shy smile and he smiled back.

Nathan was out on the dance floor, dancing with a girl she knew was called Heather. She was pretty but in a more natural way. Plus she was a nice person-Heather would be a good influence on him Isabelle thought. By the way Nathan danced with her he thought so too. Kyle looked out of place with his Emo hairstyle and his all black outfit. He almost blended into the shadows. He was sitting on the sofa with his arms crossed and was glaring at everyone. She shook her head slightly, feeling sorry for him. He needed to let go of all that anger and let the protective wall down. She could tell this wasn't his scene, but he was here all the same to support his friends which was a start. Aiden saw her looking at the dancers and mistook it for her wanting to dance, he leaned down and asked, "you want to go dance?" she looked up at him, confused.

"*I don't dance,*" she signed he chuckled and took her hand "come on, it's a party, there's **always** dancing, do you trust me?" and Isabelle nodded, "then dance with me." he said giving her that grin of his and she sighed, giving in. Aiden waved to the guys, indicating they were going to dance, Ben and Liam gave him thumbs up and Aiden shook his head at them. He led Isabelle into the dancers, and they faced each other. Isabelle looked around self-consciously and rubbed her arm.

"Hey, don't do that, you look amazing," Aiden said, and she blushed. How could he read her so well in such a short amount of time? She blushed and Aiden grinned at her. He took her hands and started swaying them, trying to get her to dance, despite feeling uncomfortable she found herself smiling at him and relented. She felt the base of the song pump through her body, vibrating in her chest and she felt herself moving to the time of the beat. This was what she missed about her past, letting herself get lost in the music the way she was now but she had to be careful-it was dangerous and she would never let herself be that self-destructive again. He grinned at her and she grinned back, blushing. They danced for what seemed like ages, her hands in his. She looked up into his face and felt her face get hot, he looked hot even in this lighting, her heart thumped in her chest not controlled by the music anymore but the look on Aiden's face. He grinned at her, and she couldn't help grinning back. She was developing feelings for him the more time she spent with him. She was playing with fire, but it was becoming harder to care about getting burnt by it. He gave her a peculiar look- as if he were about to kiss her! She swallowed but did nothing to try to stop him as his lips came closer to hers, but just as they were about to make contact there came a sharp laugh behind them.

"Aww look, it's the prince and the freak! However, did you get him to like you? Did you slip him some of your nasty love potion?" It was Stacy, she seemed to have had too much to drink and was slurring her words slightly. Her friends giggled along with her; Isabelle felt tears stung her eyes. Aiden glared at Stacy, "no one likes a bitch, Stacy, that's where Isabelle's different from you, she's not nasty. She's not fake." he said, at the mention of bitch Stacy had started to swell up like a bullfrog, her face bright red, "Excuse me?!" She shouted, "I'm fake? Really? Have you ever met the real Isabelle?" Isabelle tried tugging on Aiden's arm trying to get away, Aiden only held on tighter. "And what's that supposed to mean?" He asked his eyes two angry slits.

"It means that once upon a time, we used to be friends...only miss prissy over there decided to go all bat shit crazy and stopped talking to everyone! Not to mention the weird self-harming thing she does-" she began, and it was Isabelle's time to turn a bright shade of red. Aiden looked down at her and she looked at her feet, they didn't understand, they couldn't. She made to leave but Aiden put his arm around her, to stop her. "If-if she was self-harming then why didn't you try to help her?" Aiden asked angrily, and Stacy barked out a harsh laugh. "There's no helping her, she's tapped in the head, also it's not like we even knew about it till our argument. She'd wear long sleeves, hid it pretty well, anyway I'd have forgiven her for that, what I couldn't forgive was her going behind my back to make out with my ex-boyfriend!" She said, Aiden's arm fell slack around Isabelle, he looked down at her shocked. She pushed herself away from him, stared between Aiden and Stacy, then ran for it.

She pushed past everyone, and once she hit the front door, she ran for it. Tears streaming down her face she thought back to all that had happened. How her life had become so messed up. This was a terrible idea, why did she think that she could have a normal life? That she could have friends? That she could go to parties and be a normal teen, with normal problems. Instead her past had messed everything up and a small part of her (the small part that had been telling her this was all a bad idea from the start) whispered I told you so. She managed to run to the end of the street before she heard "Izzy! Wait!" she looked behind her, to see Aiden running after her. She had a new burst of energy and propelled herself faster, but Aiden had longer leg's and was much stronger than she was so he soon caught her up. "Stop!" he said, his hand catching around her arm, as he pulled her to a stop. She was panting and clutching at a stitch in her side, as he grabbed her up into a hug. "I'm sorry, I shouldn't have goaded her like that, I'm so sorry," he said, and she couldn't help it any longer. She broke down and started sobbing, clutching him as if he were her lifeline. As he held her, she felt the hard-lump melt in her stomach.

He had come after her, he didn't hate her! He stroked her hair and murmured to her, telling her it was ok. **I don't deserve him,** she thought. He let her pull away and he looked at her with only concern which made her sniffle, "are you ok? Shall I take you home?" He asked and she nodded, feeling tears pooling in her eyes. They started to walk again, side by side but this time in silence. He had his hands in his pockets and he looked as if he wanted to say something. She glanced up at him then looked to the floor. How did she explain what had really happened without him going totally berserk? "So..." he began, "what happened between you and Stacy?" and Isabelle took a deep breath. This was going to suck.

## CHAPTER 5. SARAH

Isabelle's palms were sweating, she didn't know what to say. Her past was so messed up she was scared he would run. *"we were primary school friends..."* she began, "*I'm sorry, it's just so...complicated,*" Aiden nodded but didn't say anything, he was going to get an explanation whether from her or not by the look of it. Isabelle sighed *"I don't know how to explain this all to you...it's a long story."* she signed and he looked down at his clasped hands. "See this photo? In my Wallet?" he asked, showing her an old photo of four people, his parents, himself and a girl. Isabelle nodded, "see the girl with brown hair next to my mum?" he asked again and Isabelle nodded not knowing where this was going.

"Her name was Sarah, my twin. She committed suicide." he said. Isabelle's eyes widened, he was talking about his twin sister, he had said she had died but she had not heard the full complete story before now. "She was being bullied, for being deaf. She couldn't talk, like you can't but sometimes when she signed, she'd make these little involuntary noises...and well the other students reacted. They laughed at her called her some horrible names. She could lip read and they knew it, but they didn't care. They went out of their way to make her life miserable. I tried to help her; I really did. I told the teachers but that made it worse. I told her to ignore them but she couldn't shut them out. I started getting into fights, which made my parents get involved, I got suspended from school...I guess she couldn't take the stress anymore. She took an overdose; paramedics couldn't save her. I knew when I found her that she was dead though. She was just so...cold..." he said. Isabelle's eyes filled with tears for him. She wrapped her arms around his waist and he gladly returned her embrace.

They stayed like this for a while until he broke away, using one hand to wipe at his face. Isabelle pretended she hadn't seen; she knew boys didn't like people seeing them crying. "So now you know..." he said, and she squeezed his hand in comfort. "Whatever happened, with Stacy, if you don't want to tell me, that's fine, but I want you to know that you're not alone," he said, and it clicked in Isabelle's head. She could see it now, why he was her friend. That maybe he saw a little of his sister in her. She wasn't going to do anything silly though, the whole reason for her silence was so she **could** live. It was time to tell him the truth. It wasn't fair to lie to him any longer, not now she knew the truth about him. Taking a deep shuddering breath, she signed *"there's something you have to know about me-"* she began but just then Aiden leaned his head down and pressed his lips to hers. The kiss wasn't long, but it was the best feeling ever. Even after Aiden pulled away her lips tingled. He looked down at her with a warm look and said "come on, it's getting late. Let's get you home." nodding Isabelle took his offered hand and they walked back in silence. Her stomach was tying itself into knots and she felt unsure as to what to do next. Life was complicated.

\*\*\*\*

The next day Aiden had turned up at the usual time outside her front door. Isabelle was nervous about being around him today, and if he were being honest Aiden was too. So much had happened in such a small amount of time that they didn't know what to say at first. Aiden babbled about anything he could think of on the drive down to fill the silence. Isabelle's father noticed giving Isabelle a questioning look but let it drop. Teenagers were always up to something (all that teenage hormones and angst. He shuddered to think…and in his opinion Aiden seemed a good boy, he could always ask Isabelle about it later.) Aiden walked her to class, as his was just up the corridor from her. "If you get any trouble, any stick off anyone, come get me, ok." He said seriously and she nodded. "Promise me?" he asked again and she nodded, blushing. She wasn't used to anyone wanting to protect her this much. Then he did something surprising, he kissed her. In front of everyone. After he pulled away, Isabelle gaped at him in shock. **What was that?** She thought. He just grinned, waved and walked down to his class, a spring in his step. Some of her classmates whispered to each other but she was too shell shocked to care, how did he keep managing to surprise her all the time? The door to her math's class opened and Mr. Parton looked out at them. "Come on you lot...in you go," the class walked in single file and took their seats ready for the register. Mr. Parton turned on the interactive white board, to show today's lesson. "Good morning class, today we will be looking at fractions, open your textbooks to pages 40, and 41..." there was the sound of shuffling of pages and suppressed groans from the class, but for once Isabelle's mind was far from thinking about fractions...

\*\*\*\*


Isabelle was on a cloud; she couldn't concentrate on any of her lessons that morning because Aiden had kissed her. He had kissed her in front of everyone, not caring what they thought, he had just done it. She felt like her heart was soaring, was she falling in love with him? Pondering that thought she didn't realize that she had walked into a trap. "Isabelle!" she was snapped out of her daydream by a familiar voice. "There you are, I wanted to ask you something," it was Josh. She groaned internally; this was the last thing she needed right now. She walked faster but ultimately, they caught her up, blocking her way forward. "Were you really at that lame party last night?" he asked and she raised a brow at him, if it were so lame then why was Stacy there? And where had he been?

"Stacy said she saw you there," he added and it made Isabelle wonder if they were on speaking terms again, whether she had forgiven him. She waited for him to say something else, not rising to the bait. She was used to people trying to force her to talk, he could literally talk to her till his face was blue and she wouldn't cave.

Taking her silence as confirmation he said "she said you were there with that new guy." he looked angry, but also hurt. Isabelle just shrugged, "Is he your boyfriend now?" He asked and again Isabelle shrugged. This seemed to infuriate him more and his hands balled into fists as he squared up to her. "Are you kidding me? Seriously?! Are you not going to say anything to me?!" He shouted "We both know you can talk, so you can just cut the cra-" CRUNCH. A fist slammed right into Josh's jaw. Josh staggered from the blow and turned to see Aiden rubbing his hand, glaring furiously. "What the HELL dude?!" Josh shouted, rubbing his smarting jaw "what was that for?" He asked. "What was that for?" Aiden asked incredulously, "you need to stop harassing Isabelle, that's what! Shouting at her like that when she's done nothing wrong! You're pathetic, picking on someone who can't fight back!" Aiden shouted. "Oh yeah?" Josh said "seems to me, she's got you wrapped right around her little finger," he lifted his pinky finger them laughed, and Aiden advanced on Josh, squaring up to him. Isabelle tried to push herself between them and started shaking her head at him, signing "*No!*" Ignoring her Aiden said "you're gonna leave her alone, no more talking to her, no more threats, if you so much as look at her-" Aiden jabbed a finger at him, threatening Josh. "Oh yeah? Are you going to stop me? Only I thought it was a free country we live in," Josh shouted back, they were starting to attract a crowd of people, who whispered and stared making Isabelle want to run and hide.

"You're a really good person, aren't you? picking on a girl who can't protect herself," Aiden sneered, Josh started clapping sarcastically. "She's got you good hasn't she?" Josh said "got you believing her 'oh, poor me, I can't talk,' crap, she's a liar, and I **will** get her to admit what she did. She's just putting this act on to make everyone feel sorry for her for what she did to Stacy," he said and Isabelle blushed, tears brimming in her eyes. So he wanted to embarrass her further did he? Shaming her here, in front of everyone? Isabelle's fist's clenched and she wanted to hit him herself. "You need to leave now before I do something I regret!" Aiden warned and Josh laughed

"you can't make me! **You don't own her,**" he said and Aiden's face flushed red "neither do you!" he growled angrily, Josh smirked "yeah? Well if Stacy hadn't interrupted us, she would have definitely been mine by now, if you know what I mean." he said turning to waggle his brows at his friends who all let out loud obnoxious laughs. Aiden retaliated, he threw another punch, and before Isabelle could blink they had begun to fight. Fists were flying as they grappled, Josh being the bigger of the two seemed to be winning, the watching crowd surged forwards to create a ring, shouting "fight! Fight!"

More added to the throng, encouraging and shouting at them, jostling Isabelle around in all the confusion. Josh grabbed Aiden in a headlock and was kicking him in the ribs when Mr. Jones the science teacher shouted: "ALRIGHT! BREAK IT UP! NOW!" He pushed into the circle and glared at the two fighting students. Grabbing each by the back of their collars he pulled them apart. "That is ENOUGH!" he shouted, his face purple with anger. "I will not have fighting on school grounds, headmaster's office, now!" he barked. Josh threw a hateful look at Aiden, wiping blood from his nose on his sleeve then he stormed over to the entrance building.

Aiden looked over apologetically to Isabelle before he set off after Josh, Mr. Jones bringing up the rear. Isabelle still had her hands over her mouth in horror as she watched them go. What had happened? She couldn't believe Aiden had fought for her, why had he done that? He had no idea what happened with Josh and Stacy, but he had defended her! One thing for certain though was that she was not about to let him get expelled because of her, even if it meant telling the truth about what happened that day. It was a few minutes before she could get her legs moving again and when she did, she hurried after them.

# CHAPTER 6. THE TRUTH.

The headmaster's office was ajar when Isabelle got there, she could see Aiden and Josh sitting in chairs in front of the headmaster's desk, neither looking at the other. Mr. Jones was gesturing wildly at the headmaster with his arms, pointing to the boys. Isabelle hesitated; she couldn't just waltz in there but she couldn't let Aiden take the blame. Noticing movement at the door, Mr. Phelps the headmaster looked up. He made a 'come here' gesture and Isabelle walked timidly into the room. She looked at Aiden who was glaring at a corner of the room, his lip bleeding. His fists were clenched on the chair arms, she saw that his knuckles were bleeding too. The sight made her heart clench, feeling like ice. This was all her fault! Aiden was hurt because of her.

"Ah, Miss Golden," Mr. Jones said "you were there weren't you? Maybe you'll tell us what went on here because these two seem to be keeping it to themselves." he said and Aiden's head whipped round. "Seriously?" he asked angrily "she **can't** talk! She does sign language for God's sake! How can she tell you what happened?" he shouted and Mr. Phelps gave him a warning glare "I suggest you lower your tone Mr. Parker," he said and Aiden folded his arms looking down. He was avoiding looking at Isabelle, which made tears brim in her eyes.

She had really done it this time, he wasn't going to want to talk to her any more...if only she could explain what had happened between her and Josh, maybe Aiden would understand. That would have to wait though, for now she had to try to get him out of trouble. "Well, maybe *you* could enlighten us as to why you were fighting?" Mr. Phelps asked him and Aiden shrugged. "You two can go wait outside. I want a word with Mr. Parker here," Mr. Phelps said and Josh stood, sending a hateful glare to Aiden he stormed out. Isabelle hesitated then signed *"I'm sorry, Aiden."* He just nodded, too angry at the moment to say anything to her.

****

Once the door was shut Mr. Phelps sighed "I really want to help you Aiden, I really do. But you're making this very difficult for me. I understand the circumstances of your past, and what has led up to here but I cannot condone fighting in my school. You do know that you're already on your final warning, you only get one chance here." Aiden just nodded. "Please, tell me why I should let you stay," he said Aiden still glared at the floor, "It must be hard losing your sister like that, and as I've always said my office is always open if you need to talk...but I really need to know what happened today. I don't want to have to expel you." Mr. Phelps asked and Aiden felt his resolve slip, he wasn't a bad guy Mr. Phelps, but he didn't know what he was going to say, he didn't really know what had happened himself.

Only that Josh was insinuating something that made his blood boil, thinking about that leeches hands all over Isabelle....it made him feel sick with anger. But it couldn't be right, could it? "Aiden?" Mr. Phelps asked and he looked up "Josh is bullying Isabelle. I told him to stop, and he said something about her-and I just snapped, Sir, it won't happen again, I promise," Aiden said. Mr. Phelps looked at him inquiringly, "you care for the girl?" he asked and after a moment of silence Aiden nodded. Sighing, Mr. Phelps said "Aiden, if what you are saying is true then this is bigger than I had thought." he said "I suppose she reminds you of your sister?" he asked and Aiden looked down at his hands and said nothing. "Isabelle is being bullied then?" he asked concerned and Aiden nodded, "It's not just Josh either, a lot of the others are mean to her too. Especially Stacy," he added, hoping that Mr. Phelps would help him protect Isabelle. "Stacy?" Mr. Phelps asked looking like he believed him.

"Stacy Wilkinson, Sir, along with Bianca Stevens and Stephanie Holland. They terrorize her sir; Josh said something really bad about her and I flipped. I'm sorry, I was only trying to protect her." Aiden said and Mr. Phelps looked thoughtful. "Thank you for your honesty, Aiden. I'll look into it." he said "this still doesn't get you out of trouble though." Aiden felt his stomach drop, he did not wish to leave the school, leave Isabelle, but Mr. Phelps just smiled. "I'm not going to expel you. But-" (Aiden smiled at him) "-I think a few week's worth of detention should do the trick. As long as you promise not to fight any more." Aiden felt his spirits lift, "I won't sir, I promise," he said and Mr. Phelps smiled back "Good. Now, go back to class, but get that lip seen to first." he said and Aiden thanked him and shut the door behind him.

That was a lucky escape, he would have to tread much more carefully from now on, he had too much to lose. Isabelle was still waiting for him outside. She looked terrified and was wringing her hands. His chest contracted, he hated seeing her like this. She looked up at him and he gave her a small smile. She sighed them flung herself at him, hugging him tight. Aiden was taken aback; she was always surprising him. She leaned back and looked him over. *"You're hurt!"* she signed and he chuckled "It's not that bad." he said and she glared at him, slapping his arm. *"You didn't have to do that!"* she scolded *"he's a jerk, but not worth getting expelled for! You scared me!"* she admitted and Aiden sighed "sorry." he said. She picked up his hand and looked at the cuts across his knuckles. "Was...was what he said true?" Aiden asked hating how vulnerable his voice had sounded. Isabelle looked up at him, tears in her eyes. *"Yes."* she signed *"But it's not what you think..."* and Aiden felt as if he couldn't breathe. "Why can't you tell me about it?" he asked and her shoulders drooped *"it's a long story, but I will tell you,"* she signed and Aiden looked hopeful. "You will?" he asked and Isabelle nodded. "Now?" he asked but Isabelle shook her head. "Tonight." she signed "Come to my house and I will tell you everything."

\*\*\*\*

Isabelle waited for Aiden to arrive with the feeling of a million tiny butterflies fluttering in her stomach. She felt sick! Her mother looked at her concernedly but she just walked away, pacing by the front door. "Is everything ok honey? You seem stressed," her mother asked and Isabelle couldn't put it off any longer. *"Aiden's coming over,"* she signed and Trish gave her a look "did something happen between you?" she asked shrewdly but Isabelle shook her head. *"No, he's coming over to do a science project with me,"* she lied her mother knew she was being untruthful but she just said "ok then hunny, is he staying for tea?" she asked, still eyeing her suspiciously. *"I don't know."* she signed after what she had to say he might never want to talk to her again. There was a knock at the door and her heart skipped a beat before thumping in her chest. She opened the door to find an equally nervous Aiden. They both hesitated before he said "Hi." Isabelle waved back at him. Noticing the awkward greeting Isabelle's mother took over. She grinned saying: "Aiden! Welcome, come on in, it's so nice to see you!" Aiden stepped over the threshold. "Hey, Mrs. Golden." Aiden said sheepishly, and she noticed his swollen and cut lip. "Are you ok, honey, did something happen," she asked concerned and Aiden blushed not knowing what to say, his own parents had been fuming with him. "I got into a fight. With Josh Newton," he admitted and Trish's eyes widened "my goodness! **why?**" she asked and he looked down at his shoe, scuffing it on the floor.

*"Josh was being mean to me,"* Isabelle supplied *"Aiden stuck up for me. He told Josh to leave me alone and they got into a fight."* she explained, and Trish's whole face warmed at this. "Well...I, thank you," she said and both teens looked at her in surprise. "You're a good boy, Aiden, looking after my girl." she said and Aiden blushed "she's lucky to have you as a friend." she gave Aiden a quick hug and then smiled at her daughter, giving her the thumbs up behind his back. "Thank you, Mrs. Golden." Aiden said embarrassed "you didn't get into too much trouble did you? Because I could have a word...I know the headmaster's wife, from church." she said and Aiden shook his head. "I got a week's worth of detention." he supplied and Trish nodded. "Good. Not that detention is good but...I'm glad you weren't expelled. Because if that man had expelled you, I'd have gone marching up that school...you mark my words." she said and Isabelle shook her head exasperation at her. "thanks Mrs.-err, I mean *Trish*," Aiden said blushing. Trish stood for a moment

looking between the two of them; looking like she was contemplating saying something before she said: "I want you to know...if you two ever decided to see each other...I wouldn't object. You're a good boy." she said and Isabelle gaped at her in shock, her mouth open. *"MUM!"* she signed; she was so embarrassing! Giving her mother an evil glare Isabelle grabbed onto Aiden's arm and steered him into the house as he laughed. *"If you're going to your room, keep the door open,"* her father signed from the kitchen as she half pulled, half dragged Aiden up the stairs. She aimed a glare at him too. This was SOOO embarrassing, she wanted to just curl up in a ball and die of shame. Why did her parents have to be like that?!

Aiden continued to chuckle for a moment. *"It's not funny!"* she signed and he held up his hands in mock surrender. "I said nothing!" he said which made her sigh, this was not his fault after all, she didn't need to take it out on him. She took him to her bedroom; it was best explained to him without 'listening ears'. She was sure her mother and father, although they liked Aiden, would probably think it too early to confide something this big to him. Ignoring her father she shut the door, partly because her father was being ridiculous and partly because if Aiden freaked out, she had a chance to calm him down before her parent's heard. She took a deep breath and faced him. He was looking around her room, and she suddenly felt shy. No boy had ever been in her room before. "It's nice," he said and she blushed, it was painted a pastel yellow, with a small bed in the middle of the room, wooden floors with a big white rug, there was a desk and computer, a small vanity with little make up and a mirror, a wardrobe and draw set. There were very little Knick knacks, except for on her bookshelf where she had little ornaments and snow globes from her holidays. "It suits you," he said and she shrugged. She sat on her bed, and patted the space next to her. Aiden went to sit next to her, curiosity evident on his face. "You said you had something you wanted to talk to me about?" he asked when it was clear she was not going to be the one to break the silence. *"Yes..."* she signed, then took another deep breath, steeling herself. *"It's about me. My family."* she began, *"we are cursed."* she said and Aiden frowned. "Cursed?" he asked and she looked down, stroking out the creases on her bedspread.

*"Yes."* she answered *"a long time ago, my great, great, great grandfather angered a gypsy woman, and she cursed our family line. Every time we talk, this happens-"* she lifted the sleeve of her jumper to show him the scars on her arm. His eyes widened and he let out a little pained noise, he reached down and stroked one of the lines. "So...it's true, what they said was true." he said softly and she looked up at him, *"someone told you about these?"* she asked fearing what he was going to say, but knowing all along that people had seen it all the same that night everything went wrong. "Stacy said..." he hesitated and Isabelle nodded for him to continue, "she said that you did this to yourself. That she saw them,

that's what everyone says about you. That you self-harm. That you carve words onto your skin or something." he explained, not looking at her.

Isabelle felt her face burn, angry tears burning in her eyes, **so she told the whole school did she?** She looked at Aiden, did he believe in what he had heard? "You need to talk to someone about this, it's not healthy. I want you to know, you're not on your own any more, I'll be here, no matter-" he began, talking to her earnestly, taking her hands in his own. She snatched them back, *"wait! you think...? I did not do this! Did you not hear what I just told you?"* she signed and he gave her a wary look, "Isabelle-" he began and she snorted *"you believe I could do something like this."* she asked and he looked panicked, conflicted. *"I'm cursed! This is a curse!"* She signed and he gave her a pained expression "yes, it can be a curse, but there's people out there who can-" he tried. Isabelle shook her head at him *"I did not do this to myself! I can prove it!" she signed angrily "Look!"* She lifted her arm, and concentrating on the clear space on her arm she cleared her throat and said, "Stop."

Her voice sounded scratchy and hoarse with not talking for such a long. The words instantly etched into her arm, blood seeping out of the cut. Aiden Jumped up in shock, then stared down at it, at first in silent disbelief and then as the colour drained from his face leaving it grey, he swayed slumping back onto the bed. "Jesus!" he said softly, leaning forwards to rest his head in his hands.

"Jesus!" he repeated, Isabelle tapped his shoulder, and he looked up at her. *"Aiden?"* she signed and he took a shaky breath. "So...a, a curse did this?" he asked stuttering and she nodded, feeling like this was a bad idea. "Ok." he nodded back. They sat in silence for a while, until he asked "what, what does the curse do?" he asked he sounded much calmer and she felt a small bit of relief settle into her stomach. *"Whenever I talk out loud, words appear on my skin. It will eventually cover almost my whole body,"* she explained and he frowned. "What happens when you run out of space?" he asked. *"I die."* she signed.

\*\*\*\*

Isabelle watched Aiden's face as he processed what she had told him. He was taking it fairly well, she had expected him to scream, or run, or something like that. But he had sat, and listened to everything she had to say about the curse. "So, your dad is the same?" he asked and she nodded *"yes. And he has less space than me, now."* she signed and he reached up to give her hand a squeeze. "Why does Stacy hate you? And what has it got to do with Josh? Did they see your scars?" Aiden asked, and Isabelle ducked her head. "*It's kind of to do with the curse, it's something I'm not very proud of.*" She began:

*"A year back, I sort of went through a faze, kind of rebelling against the curse, I used to talk a lot, that's why I have a lot of scars. I got into the wrong crowd. I started staying out late, going to parties all the time. Drinking. This one party, I was totally drunk. I was so drunk that I allowed Josh to kiss me. He was Stacy's boyfriend, she was my best friend and I was too drunk to care. I hated the world and the world hated me. So I kissed him back, and Stacy walked in on us...the rest is history. I got home somehow and my parents found me, drunk and sick as a dog. The looks on their faces...they were beyond disappointed. They were scared for me. After that I had a wake up call, my self destruction was only hurting them, and whatever pain I was feeling-they were feeling it too only much worse, and it wasn't fair. So I stopped talking, the school had already found out what I had done so everyone hated me, the 'slag' and it was easy to be ignored so I never really wanted to talk again."* she signed., Aiden nodded, wrapping an arm around her shoulder.

They stayed like that, their heads resting against each other, listening to the wind on the windows. At one point he had taken her hand into one of his own, reaching up to touch the silvery words at the base of her wrist with a fingertip. "Does it hurt?" he asked as he traced a scar, *"yes, sometimes, I try not to talk if I can help it. Laughing counts, so I have to be careful whatever noise I make."* she signed. Aiden took her hand again after she finished her signing. It was like he had to hold onto her, to reassure himself that she was real, that this was real. "Is there a cure?" he asked and she shrugged.

*"My family has been searching for a cure for years. We've searched every book, artefact you could think of, nothing has worked. My great grandfather's thought was that if we could find the gypsy colony who cursed us, that someone will know how to cure us,"* she signed and Aiden's face lit up. "Does he still have the research?" he asked and she hesitated. *"Yes. But I don't think we found anything. My father just stopped looking one day. Just out of the blue, and when I asked him about it, he just said to leave it. That it was all a dead end."* Aiden frowned at this, then said "maybe...I could help?" he asked and it was Isabelle's turn to frown, *"how?"* she asked and he grinned "I can take a look, if you want? Have an outsiders point of view? Plus, we can go down to the library, I'll bet they have records of this sort of thing, and there's the internet," he said and she felt the knot of dread loosen in her stomach, he believed her! And even better, he wanted to help her! He was such a good person.

*"You're an amazing person, you know that right?"* she asked and he blushed. "Nah," he said shaking his head "I'm just trying my best to help out a friend in a terrible situation. *You're* the amazing person for going through all this on your own." he said looking into Isabelle's eyes, there was a sudden tension in the air, and Isabelle felt her heart begin to speed up again, thumping hard in her

chest. Not out of fear this time, but with something else. He leaned in closer, his mouth inches from her own- "I thought you'd like some-oh!" Trish had banged open the door which made both teens jump away from each other, her mother stared at them for a moment before a grin lit up her face "sorry, I'll just...I'll go. Here," she placed a plate of cookies on the desk, then left the room with a smug grin on her face. Isabelle made a noise of annoyance and hid her head in her hands as Aiden laughed. **Why was her parents so annoying?** She thought despairingly. "Shall we get on with our homework before your mother has an aneurysm?" Aiden joked and Isabelle sighed, nodding as she pulled her bag closer to her. Even if her mother had walked in on them nearly kissing, it couldn't dampen her good mood for long because Aiden believed her, and wanted to help her. Life was looking up for a change.

# CHAPTER 7. INTENSIVE CARE

The next couple of weeks went by in a blur. They spent so much time together people were joking that they were joined at the hip. It was also common knowledge around the school that they were dating. Although they hadn't put a label on what it was that was going on between them, there was still a closeness that was more than friendship. Aiden would hold her hand when they walked, and would surprise her with a kiss to the forehead that made Isabelle believe that he liked her more than a friend, and that she did too. It was fine with her, taking this slow, not putting a name to their relationship, with how complicated things were, and she was grateful to him for that. People seemed to be a lot kinder to her when Aiden was around, and instead of people whispering bad things about her, they only had good things to say about her. A girl had even complimented her long hair! Aiden had changed her life completely, in the best way possible.

They also spent a lot of time together up in the attic, looking through her father's research. It was only a small room, with low beams and dark wood. Piled on top of each other were boxes and boxes of books on the Occult, home remedy spell books that turned out to be gimmicks, one box labelled 'DO NOT TOUCH-CURSED OBJECTS' that they had skirted around, file upon file of paper trails for different gypsy camps and colonies. There was a spider diagram on the wall filled with string and pins attaching drawings and photographs to it, that didn't make all that much sense. One word that stood out among the research was this: Vanslow It was the last name of the traveler woman who had cursed the family, all that long ago. Aiden had first gone to the library to find anything that sounded like it fitted with the colony that the Boswell's were linked to, and he had methodically photocopied and attached it to the diagram in hopes to bring some light to their own research. Isabelle's hopes seemed to dwindle as Aiden seemed more and more determined that they would find something. "It's only a matter of time," he told her "they can't have just disappeared. We'll find something, you'll see."

At the end of another dull school morning, Isabelle waited for Aiden in their usual spot when she got the phone call. She looked down at the caller ID, thinking it was just another PPI nuisance call planning to end it, but instead the word 'MUM' appeared on screen. She frowned down at the screen, why was her mother calling her? Her mother never called, unless...she swiped across to answer the call and lifted the phone to her ear. "Isabelle? Thank goodness! I've been trying to call the school but there's been no answer!" Trish said, sounding frantic, and Isabelle felt her heart clench, this did not sound good. "It's, oh honey, it's your dad!" she said, her voice sounding thick with tears and Isabelle gasped, "he's been rushed to hospital, they won't say what's wrong other than he collapsed during a police interview," she said and tears welled up in Isabelle's eyes, why was he in a police station? She thought and it hit her. He must have spoken, that's why he collapsed, he's going to die! It took her a few moments before she realised her mother was still talking "...going down there now! Can you go to the office, get one of the teachers to drop you off? It-it doesn't sound good, baby. You need to hurry." she said and Isabelle let out a sob, not really feeling the stinging burn as it cut into her skin. "Oh honey...don't cry. Just-just hurry, ok?" she said and then hung up. Isabelle still had her phone to her ear, in shock when Aiden ran over.

He was grinning, holding a piece of paper when she saw him, and he said "We had a free period and I did some research online-I think I found something, here, look. There's a marriage listed here between a Lavinia Vanslow, to a Thomas Boswell. Their colony is listed here. I think we found them!" he said, showing her the sheet of paper. Isabelle looked down at it blankly. He noticed the horror written on her face and his own grin turned to fear. "Isabelle...what is it? What's wrong?" he asked, taking her shoulders in his hands. She looked up at him, her expression frightened and she signed *"it's my dad."* She then burst into tears; Aiden then wrapped his arms around her. "What happened? Is he ok? Please, talk to me!" He said trying to console her. He pulled back to look into her eyes, "tell me so I can help," he said and after taking a few gulps of air Isabelle signed *"he is in hospital, my mum just called, she wants me to go down to the office to see if anyone will take me, she said it's not looking good..."* she explained tears still streaming down her face. "Ok, let's go down now then, I'll stay with you." He said, putting an arm around her to support her they made their way quickly to the office. When the door opened the secretary looked up then exclaimed "Goodness! Whatever's the matter!" She walked out of the work bench to put an arm around the other side of Isabelle who was still crying.

"It's her dad..." Aiden explained "her mum just called there's been some sort of accident and he's in the hospital," he said as they all sat down on the waiting chairs, and Lynne the receptionist said "oh you poor thing!" she patted her arm consoling. "Is someone coming to get you?" she asked and Isabelle shook her head, her mother and father had been only children and her grandparents were either too far away or dead. "Do you want to stay here until someone is free to come and get you? You can use the office phone and make a phone call," she said helpfully but Isabelle shook her head. "No?" Lynne asked, confused. "I don't think anyone can come get her, Miss." Aiden said, *"my mother told me to ask if one of the teachers could take me,"* she signed at him and Aiden nodded "Her mum wanted her to ask if one of the other teachers could take her," Aiden supplied but Lynne shook her head. "I'm sorry honey, but that's not possible, if they're late coming back for lessons then it affects the other student's," she said apologetically, which made Isabelle cry harder, feeling helpless.

Aiden had a brainwave, "hey, my dad's working from home today, I could call him, ask him if he could take you?" he said and Isabelle looked up at him with hope in her eyes, *"He would do that?"* she asked, her hands shaking as she signed. Aiden noticed and gave her a small smile "he'd do anything for you, Izzy," he said and she wrapped her arms around him, Lynne smiled at them before she said "you can use the office phone," when he moved away to call his dad, Lynne turned to Isabelle and said "he's a keeper, that one. Hold on tight now, don't let him slip through your fingers." with a wink and Isabelle stared at Aiden nodding. He really was a keeper. After saying goodbye to his father, he turned and said "he's on his way now," and Isabelle stood to wrap her arms around his neck, gratefully.

"I'm coming too," he said "you're not going to be alone," he said and she shook her head, "no. I'm coming. This is more important than school at the moment," he said and she sighed. He knew her so well; she had been worrying about him falling behind on work. They sat there for a while, his arm wrapped around her shoulder as she rested her head against his neck, seeking comfort. Aiden's father marched in a moment after, out of breath and concerned, he looked at the two of them and stopped. He arched an eyebrow at his son but said nothing, "are you ready to go?" he asked Isabelle who looked up with puffy eyes. She nodded and made to go when Lynne said "I've made excuses to your teachers, you won't be expected back today, I hope your father is ok," she said and Isabelle nodded gratefully at her, signing thank you.

Keeping a firm arm around her Aiden set his jaw, knowing what was coming. "You should go back to class, Aiden," his father said but Aiden just shook his head, "I'm not leaving her, she needs me." he had that determined look that his father knew there was no point arguing, he was after all his mother's son and stubbornness was in his DNA. Sighing, Mr. Parker shook his head. "Ok, but I expect you to catch up on all missed work," he said and with a nod, they left for the car park. The drive was silent, so many things unspoken that whirled around in Isabelle's head. She looked down and picked at the stitching on her coat, a nervous habit. Seeing Isabelle's hand picking apart the seams of her coat, Aiden reached over and covered it, "he's going to be ok," Aiden promised, and Isabelle stopped her picking to wrap her fingers in his, not releasing how cold she felt until his hand warmed her own. If only she believed that it was true, she thought as tears blurred her vision.

\*\*\*\*

The beep, beep of the monitor machine was only a little reassuring as Isabelle stared down at her father. His face looked pale and waxy, as if he had already gone. There were many tubes and cables attaching him to many things that were momentarily keeping him alive, but the nurses and doctors were stumped as to why his stats were constantly dropping. They also had many questions about the scars that Trish could not answer for fear of him being taken away to some crazy experimental lab. He had been placed into a coma for now, and it was just a waiting game, to see if he would pick up or not. Isabelle looked up at her mother, who was holding onto his hand, tears making their way down her cheeks.

"He's going to be ok, he'll...he'll wake up, you'll see..." she said hopefully, she was stroking a small sentence on his hand, it said 'I do'. Their love for one another etched right there on his skin, their wedding vows. Isabelle nodded reaching over to take his other hand in both of hers. It was still warm. They stayed like that for a while before a doctor came in and wanted to talk to her mother on her own. She hesitated at the door, she wanted to hear it too, wanting to support her mother. But Trish just nodded at her to go on with a brave smile, so Isabelle left the room. Out in the corridor she started to pace, wringing her hands as all the new worries and thoughts swam around in her head. He couldn't die! They both needed him, he was their rock, a calm, reassuring, dependable man...he could not leave them! This was how Aiden found her, he came around the corridor with two Starbucks coffee cups, he rushed to her and wrapped his arms around her, careful not to spill the hot liquid. He guided her to the seats opposite the door and gave her one of the cups, "here, this will help you feel better," he said but she couldn't bring herself to drink it with her stomach churning, she held onto it though, letting it warm her. She brought a shaky hand up to her chin and signed *"Thank you,"* Aiden smiled sympathetically then they fell into silence. Once or twice Aiden opened his mouth to say something, but closed it feeling as if he were intruding on her grief. The doctor opened the door, his back to them, and said "if you need anything, the nurses will be glad to help," he said and they heard Trish say "thank you doctor," he let the door swing shut and walked away down the corridor.

Both Isabelle and Aiden stood and went back into the room, Isabelle rushing to her mother's side. She wrapped her arms around her, and Aiden was left to take the empty chair on Mr. Goldens' other side. "What did he say?" he asked as he looked at the grieving pair. Trish took a gulp of air, trembling and she said "he-he said, that he doesn't know why but kidneys and liver seem to be shutting down, it's like...like his body is giving up. They've given him injections, and they're keeping his fluids up. He's on a dialysis machine, but..." she shrugged "they're not very hopeful he'll get better on his own," she said as tears rolled down her face, she hiccupped. "I'm sorry..." Aiden said not knowing what to say, he had lost his sister but it was not like this. It was different because for now he was still here, still holding on if only for the moment. What did you say to someone who knew the inevitable was coming? Looking at him, lying there, with all of those scars covering his body, bandages and tubes around him-it was like looking into the future, he saw Isabelle lying there instead, the ventilator tube in **her** mouth instead her fathers....

*"Why did the police arrest him?"* Isabelle asked, tears streaming down her cheeks. "There was some sort of tip off, apparently. Someone had said he was selling drugs at the school...I don't know why someone would say such a thing, what they could possibly gain from this..." her mother said falteringly, with thick emotion in her voice. Suddenly Isabelle's blood started to boil, she **knew** who had tipped off the police off. Knew who would gain something from such a terrible thing. *"Josh."* She signed looking towards Aiden, his eyes widened then he looked angry, very angry. "That-That son of a bitch!" He struggled to get out his sentence "I'm going to kill him! I'm going to ring his neck!" He shouted balling up his fists. Trish looked from one teen to the other. "What is it? What's going on?" She asked.

"The one person who stands to gain from something like this?" Aiden said through slit eyes "it's Josh, the guy who's been bullying Izzy, he thinks she belongs to him somehow, she chose me over him now he wants her to pay," he supplied and Trish's eyes went round. "A boy did this...a school boy," she shook her head. "He won't get away with this..." Aiden said Darkly. "No. Whatever you're planning, don't. We need a low profile, what's happened to Matthew...it's not normal, we don't want more attention brought over here. Look at his mark's, tell me it's not something the news would be interested in, the government...I'll not have him experimented on. You need to drop this. Now." She warned, both of them nodded. *"What do we do,"* Isabelle asked, "you act normal. You go to school, do your homework, don't draw any attention to yourselves..." she said, with those instructions Aiden gasped, it was as if a light switch had been thrown in his brain! The research!

He leaned down and reached into his back, his hand scrabbling around, looking...he pulled out the paper and held it up, his eyes reading. The two women watched with detached curiosity, what was he doing? "Izzy," he said his voice with growing excitement, "before, you told me about your father was hurt, I found something," he said and Isabelle looked sharply at him, concentrating hard on the hopeful expression on his face. "I did some more research, I think I found them." he said and Isabelle let go of her mother to walk around to him, **did he really mean...?** She thought, her own hopes lifting. "Here," he said, handing over the paper, she read through quickly, her own excitement and hope building inside her. Was this what they had been hoping for this whole time? "What is it honey?" her mother asked and Isabelle looked to Aiden to explain. "You sure?" he asked her and she nodded, it was time her mother knew. "Isabelle told me about the curse." he began, and Trish looked shocked at her daughter. "I know everything, how they were cursed, what happens when they talk, about how it kills them...she showed me her father's research. We've been doing our own research. I...I think I found them. The gypsy colony, the one where the witch lady came from," he said and Trish gasped "you found them?" she asked and Aiden nodded as Isabelle gave her mother the paper to read.

"London?" she asked squinting at the paper, "they're in **London**? That close by, after all that time?" she said as she looked first at the marriage papers then the gypsy listings. "We could go," Aiden offered, and both girls shook their heads looking at Matthew (Mr. Golden) who's monitors continued to beep. "Wait, listen, we could go-Isabelle and I-and find them, bring them here to heal him, ask them to break the curse!" Aiden said and Isabelle looked up at him with surprise. *"I can't ask you to do that, you don't have to do anything."* Isabelle signed and he gave her a small smile. "Yes I do. You helped me when I was new here, helped me settle in and let go of the past. I owe you...and I-I love you." he said, Isabelle stared at him, her mouth popping open like some sort of stunned unattractive goldfish. **He loved her?!** He had really just said it? He looked embarrassed and was blushing as she continued to stare gob smacked. "Say something?" he said and she closed her mouth standing to hug him close. She looked up into his face and signed *"I love you too."* which was true, she had been falling for him from day one. He leaned down to kiss briefly, which warmed Isabelle slightly before they turned to her mother who watched them. She turned her gaze to her husband, watching his sleeping face. "It's too dangerous," she said her voice flat and Isabelle glared at her. *"Not if it saves dad,"* she signed and her mother reached up to rub her forehead, not seeing her daughter's argument but knowing she wouldn't agree. "Even if you found them, there's no guarantee of them knowing anything about the curse." her mother said, sounding defeated. "But-" Isabelle tried to argue, "Izzy...don't." Aiden warned and her mother gave him a small smile. "You understand? It's not worth you two getting hurt. There was a reason Matthew stopped searching, just...promise me you won't go looking for them." she begged. "Isabelle?"

Isabelle looked down at her feet, but nodded. There was no point arguing, her mother would not be persuaded. "Let's go get something to eat." he suggested and Isabelle allowed herself to be led out. Isabelle took one last look through the door before it swung shut. She was not going to let her father die! *"We have to go!"* she signed to Aiden, "but your mother-" he began *"she can't stop me. I'll go with or without your help."* she warned, her jaw set with determination. Aiden signed and said "ok. But, let's do it properly. We'll need supplies: clothes, food, money." he said and so they started to make a plan.

## CHAPTER 8. LONDON

Aiden got his dad to drop them off at Isabelle's house, where they told him they would get some food and pack a hospital bag for her mother. Instead they rushed around packing a bag for Isabelle. Aiden went on the computer to book train tickets for London, Kensal green in Middlesex. That was where Lavinia Boswell was settled, a descendant of the gypsy woman who cursed the family all those years ago. Once they were certain they had everything that they needed from Isabelle's house they set off for his house. Isabelle waited while Aiden packed his school bag with clothes and money, Aiden's excuse was that he was going to stay at Isabelle's house to offer support for her and her mother in their time of need and his father reluctantly agreed he could go. It wasn't like Aiden to lie about things, which made it all the harder to do what they had to. It was coming up to 6:00 when they arrived at the train station via taxi, and Isabelle's nerves were writhing around in her stomach.

She had never done anything like this before, they were for all intent and purpose, running away from home. She paced the platform, wringing her hands and looking nervous. Aiden grabbed her arm and pulled her close to him. "Hey," he said "it's going to be ok," he stroked her hair, trying his best to comfort her when his own insides felt like a bag of snakes wriggling around. *"I can't stand lying to them,"* she signed and Aiden gave her a ghost of his usual smile "they will understand. We're not doing anything wrong." he said. Their train left at half six, not that long from now but Isabelle willed the train to come sooner. She felt like she was a naughty school girl, standing there like they were. She felt as if every eye turned their way was an accusing one, like they knew what they were up to but that was just silly, no one knew why they were there. They probably stared because she was using sign language like she was sometimes used to happening, plus Aiden was right, they weren't technically doing anything wrong. She took a deep calming breath and relaxed a little.

"There, that's better," Aiden said "you keep acting shifty and they'll know something's up. Then we wouldn't be able to get on the train." he said. "We're doing this for your dad, just think about that." He wrapped an arm around her shoulders and Isabelle sighed nodding, relaxing back to snuggle into Aiden's arms. He kissed the top of her head and they waited. When the train arrived they hurried on and claimed some chairs to the back of the compartment. Easier to sit close to the doors so they could jump off quickly. Isabelle rested her head on Aiden's shoulder and closed her eyes, feeling suddenly very tired as the weight of the past couple of days crashed down on her. Feeling comforted by the gentle rock of the train carriage and the thought that they were going to save her dad made a small beam of hope blossom in her chest. She felt her eyes getting heavy as she leaned against Aiden and before she knew it she was fast asleep.

****

"Izzy...?" The voice said, puncturing the warm fog of sleep. "Izzy...time to wake up, we're here." Aiden said, shaking her shoulder slightly. Isabelle opened her eyes and sat up. Yawning and rubbing her eyes she noticed that indeed they had stopped. "Come on," Aiden said leaving his seat and donning his rucksack. Isabelle followed him, feeling stiff from sleeping on the train seats. They left the train and walked away into the crowd. The station was pretty small, with a coffee shop and restrooms along with the ticket box. This was just a stop until they could get their next train. Since they had half an hour, they went to the restrooms to freshen up and bought drinks at the coffee shop. They took their hot beverages to the platform they needed and sat, waiting. *"Thank you for helping me,"* Isabelle said, feeling mixed emotions. "You'd do the same for me." He said warmly, she remembered the kiss and the way he had said I love you and she blushed.

**When this was all over,** Aiden thought **I'll take her on a real date.** They stared at each other a heartbeat longer before Isabelle raised her cup and took a sip. Yum. She much preferred hot chocolate over coffee. Coffee was bitter. "So... what do you think Lavinia will say...?" Aiden said a little awkwardly, Isabelle shrugged. *"I just hope she knows about all this stuff."* She signed instead, "I think most Romany gypsies know a little witchcraft." Aiden said and Isabelle tried not to choke on her sip of hot chocolate. *"That is just plain racist,"* she signed taking out the sting of the words with a smile. "No, they do know magic. I went to a fair once, and saw a fortune teller, she was a gypsy lady. She did my cards and she told me I have a destiny, that I would meet a golden-haired woman who would need my protection." He said "she said I'd give my heart to her...she was talking about you." He blushed, Isabelle blushed too. *"So you think Lavinia can really help us?"* She asked and Aiden smiled "I do." He said with conviction. Isabelle's phone rang, making her jump. Oh no....she thought, her mother. She picked up the phone with wide eyes and handed it to Aiden. "Oh no, I'm not talking to her," he said his hands up. She waggled the phone at him not giving up and he sighed. "Hello?" He asked it, and instantly was bombarded with a hysterical voice. "Ok, ok, calm down Mrs. Golden, she's with me." He said and Isabelle fidgeted feeling guilty, her mother didn't need the added stress. But again, she couldn't let her father just die. "Yeah, she's ok...I'm sorry, but I don't think she'll come home...I understand that but she loves her father...yeah, ok," he covered the mouth piece, saying "she wants to speak to you." Isabelle sighed but nodded, reaching her hand out so she could take the phone. She pressed it to her ear expecting a shouting match but she was surprised when she heard her mother's voice. "Isabelle...?" Came her mother's trembling voice, "please come home," she begged "you can't help your father this way, no good will come out of it, baby. Please come home, I need you..." she sounded like she was crying, and Isabelle let out a small sob. She was hurting her mother. "Isabelle?" She asked and Isabelle sniffed, she hated that she was hurting her but images of her father in the hospital bed flashed across her mind. With a growing resolve she moved the phone away from her face and ended the call. "Izzy?" Aiden asked and she shook her head, crying silently. She didn't want to talk about it. He just reached over and wrapped an arm around her. She leaned into him gratefully, resting her head on his shoulder. He kissed the top of her head, "we'll figure this out, I promise." He said.

****

She couldn't sleep the rest of the train ride, she felt keyed up and on edge. She wanted to pace, to wring her hands and dissolve into a puddle of stress but they were on a train and it would be hard to do. Not to mention that it would draw unwanted attention. Aiden had let his head loll back and was soon softly snoring, she glanced at him and smiled a little. She was lucky to have him, he was such a good, honest person. He looked adorable asleep and something in the image of him this soft and vulnerable settled the turmoil in her heart and her head enough that she could sit and wait calmly. There was nothing they could do about it now, anyway. Her phone went off again and she glanced at the caller ID, her mother. Pushing away the feeling of guilt she turned off her phone for a while, she couldn't talk to her again and hear the pleading and the stress in her mother's voice, it would weaken her resolve. She stared out of the window and watched as the towns turned to fields then back to towns again. When the train stopped in London station Isabelle shook Aiden's shoulder, he blinked and looked around. "We're here?" He asked groggily and she nodded.

They left the train and stood outside the huge London Underground train station, "wanna go to the hotel take a nap and freshen up or go find Lavinia first?" Aiden asked, she bit her lip and thought for a while. On the one hand Aiden looked beat, and she felt bad she was dragging him along for this but on the other hand she knew she wouldn't be able to sleep until this was all over. He could see her internal struggle and said "you wanna try get this over with quickly? Let's go see if we can find Lavinia first then we can eat then go sleep after. Deal?" He asked, she nodded gratefully. "Ok," he grinned "let's get a taxi there, be easier than wandering around for a while getting lost," he threw an arm around her shoulder, and she nuzzled into him feeling some of the tension leave her. Aiden held up a hand to flag one of the taxis, those big black ones that seemed to be everywhere. One stopped for them and Aiden told him where to go, using the print off as a guide. When they were rolling away from the curb Aiden said happily, "I've always wanted to go in one of these," he looked around him taking it all in. *"What are these things anyway,"* she signed and Aiden grinned "a TX 1, they're the standard taxi brand for London." He supplied and she grinned back *"they remind me of a bug, like a shiny beetle,"* she said. Aiden chuckled at that and they settled back to enjoy the view.

## CHAPTER 9. THE CARAVAN.

Wormwood scrubs park-Isabelle decided-was a very *strange* area for the gypsies to choose as for their temporary caravan site (although back home the travelers who sometimes went through chose some strange spots for example the Morrison's car park they decided to stay for a couple of weeks one year, or the children's park which was almost as small as this one, they had driven onto the walking pathway, and parked on the grass, which made the locals grumble until the police had asked them to leave.) Most had taken up camp in the car park, though she could see some tents set up on the grass.

There was a sign stating the price of using the car park, £2.20 an hour, minimum charge £1.10, but she supposed that they probably weren't paying to stay there. She shrugged, **still…it wasn't any of her business,** she thought. The cab driver parked just outside the park, on the curb and Aiden paid the overly priced cab fair. "We should have just taken the tube to Kensal green, and walked." he continued to grumble. *"Well at least we know for next time,"* Isabelle soothed him. "If there is a next time…" he said still grumbling about the cost, they stood back and took in the scene. This wasn't one of those permanent caravan pitches where the gypsy's (or travelers as they were called sometimes) were allowed to settle. Also this particular group were of the few gypsy's that still travelled around- they seemed to stick to the same route as Aiden had found out on line, lucky for them...so it was hard enough to track them but Aiden had managed it by using a website. It was only a small caravan of travelers so it wasn't too difficult to find them and after a few phone calls he had managed to track them down to here (though they wouldn't stay at this park for much longer.)

They started to walk into the car park, towards the travelers, not sure what to expect. There were a lot of different types of caravans, some had those small drivable caravans and some had attached to car's the type of caravan she and her family holidayed in in Wales. Then there were the traditional Romany caravans, they were the most beautiful looking caravans Isabelle had ever seen. There were only two of them but they drew the eye with their magnificent colours. They were obviously horse drawn and two big horses were tethered to the sides munching on bags of hay. The closest caravan was round shaped and a bright green with gold filigree in the shape of leaves; the other square shaped one was a bold red colour, edged with fancy looking swirling gold filigree. A huge chestnut coloured shire horse was eating from a bale of hay tied to the side of the green caravan. On the red one a white and brown patched Draft horse munched, his blue eyes watching them curiously. An old woman sat outside on a wooden chair, knitting. *"Is that her?"* Isabelle asked with sign language though she supposed that she didn't really need to any more if that really was her. "Could be...lets go ask," Aiden said and they walked over to her, their shoulders brushing, taking comfort and bravery from the touch. "Um.... are you Lavinia Bosswell?" Aiden asked nervously, the old woman looked up with slightly cataract eyes, she seemed *very* old. Her skin was a lovely bronze colour, though it was saggy and wrinkled with age, looking kind of papery and veiny. Her white hair was tied back in a bun, and she wore a long blue patterned skirt with a white blouse. A pink crochet shawl lay around her shoulders that she obviously made herself, it looked as if she were making a new one, this in an olive green colour. She looked the teens up and down before pointing at a sign at the door. It was a business sign saying:

### THE GREAT LAVINA,

### Fortune teller,

Tarot reading, crystal ball, tea leaves, palm reading.

Under this was a list of times of the day she did her 'business'. Aiden looked at his watch and groaned. Today said 10:00 am, it was still only 9:30. He turned to Isabelle who shrugged. "We're not here for a reading Mrs. Bosswell," Aiden said but she just pointed to the sign, not even bothering to look up from her knitting. Isabelle tugged at the shoulder of his denim jacket and he looked at her. *"It's fine, we can wait,"* she signed, Lavinia looked up and squinted at Isabelle to watch her use sign language. She contemplated the new customers; she sensed an urgency and hopelessness about the boy but found she was for once stumped when it came to the girl. She was very hard to read. Sighing to herself, she stood on shaky legs, her hips weren't what they used to be and after grabbing a cane she shuffled to the caravan. She looked back at the young couple and said: "Come." she turned and walked up the stairs, parting the beaded curtain to enter within. Aiden and Isabelle looked at each other in nervous anticipation. "Come on," he said taking her hand to lead her through. It was small inside the caravan and quite cluttered.

There was a tiny bed built into the back with lavender patterned covers and pillows. A plush pink armchair sat pushed up to the side, in front was a small round table with tablecloth, then two hard backed chairs were positioned on the opposite side of the comfy looking chair. The walls were a bright sunny yellow, a small dresser, a tiny camping hob with copper pots and pans hanging on the walls above...there really wasn't too much room to move around in but there seemed to be a huge number of candles, ornaments and lace doilies. It would have seemed a normal if cluttered place but there were also very strange things integrated with the everyday objects, like the ropes of lavender and sage smudge sticks hanging down from a hook in the corner, a crystal ball sat in the center of the table. A shelf containing normal looking herbs, spices and pickled....*things*. Shuddering, Isabelle tried not to look too closely at those. There was also a painted poster of a woman on the wall that had three eyes, one directly in the middle of her forehead. Lavinia took the soft armchair and motioned for them to take the wooden chairs opposite. Feeling nervous they sat and stared about them. "£10," the old woman said, holding out an age-spotted hand, Aiden looked at her confused.

"What?" he asked and she shook her hand at them again. "£10, then we begin," she said and after shrugging at each other, Isabelle took out a crisp ten pound note out of her purse to give to the old woman. She turned to the shelf and pulled a wooden box from the bottom shelf. She took out her tarot cards and placed them in front of her. She pulled out matches and lit a fat pillar candle, she lowered her head and muttered to it. "Spirits of my ancestors," she said in a thick Romany accent "protect us from any evil that wishes to intrude on our reading," she crossed herself in the catholic sign of the cross, blessing herself. That's when they noticed the rosary around her neck, Aiden looked at Isabelle and mouthed 'huh' at her, wondering if a devout catholic could also be a medium? After kissing the silver cross on her rosary she picked up the cards. She handed them to Isabelle, and mimed that she should shuffle them. "Ma'am she's not deaf," Aiden said which earned him a beady eyed look. She held out her hand to him as Isabelle shuffled. He thought she wanted to shake hands, so he took hers only for her to grasp his hand in both of hers so she could turn it palm up. "You have a good, strong life line, you will only love once, but it will be a hard road to follow..." she said looking at the lines on his hand, "you have suffered a loss...you feel responsible somehow...but you must not dwell on it. She is at peace." she said nodding "you will have 2 children; you will name your daughter Millie...after your sister. You will be happy..." she smiled warmly at him, letting go so he could take his hand back. Aiden looked at her a little afraid. *How could she know all those things?* He thought to himself.

"That will be enough," she said to Isabelle as she shuffled the cards. "Split it into three columns," she asked her, and Isabelle complied. "Past, present and future," The old woman said then she picked up each, stacking them in her hands. She started to put the cards out in front of Isabelle, right side up, she studied the pictures. "You have had a very hard life; you suffer yet you don't give up. You are a very strong character, with a good heart." she said then she put another three cards down. "You made a mistake; you rebelled and paid a price for it. But this does not mean that you are a bad person, like you think it does. It means you made a mistake but that you learned from it. If not for those mistakes...you would not have this boy at your side today. Everything happens for a reason, child. You came here to ask something of me...a favor." she smiled kindly, she glanced down at the new cards she placed there. The next three cards must have come as a shock to the old woman, her eyes widened and looked up to Isabelle. In the center was the death card. Isabelle felt her own eyes glued to the other. She saw fear there.

Suddenly she reached forwards and yanked up Isabelle's sleeve, looking at the markings there and the extent of the curse, she snatched back her hand and crossed herself again, muttering in her mother tongue a prayer before facing the two again. "Out." Lavinia said, her voice hoarse. "What?" Aiden said confused "Out! Get out! OUT!" the old woman shouted, standing up quickly so she could shoo at them. "But...*Please,* we need your help!" Aiden begged. "Nu te pot ajuta! I cannot help you! Go! Get out of my caravan!" she shouted fearfully. "We need a cure, her father is going to *die* if you don't help!" Aiden pleaded as she continued to shoo them, shuffling at them so as to force them out. "Nu te pot ajuta! Go please!" she looked terrified and Isabelle felt her heart turn to ice, this woman would not help them, her father was doomed.

"We just need the spell. The cure, you don't have to be involved, just give us the cure," Aiden shouted as they were forced to walk out and down the stairs. "*Este o vraja rea*! It is...*evil* spell! I cannot help you, I'm sorry," she said and with a bang, she shut the door on them. Isabelle looked at Aiden crestfallen, had they had come all this way....for nothing? She wasn't going to help them, that much was clear. But she knew of the curse, and even of a cure. She had said it was evil. Why? Shaking his head Aiden motioned her to come over, so he could wrap his arms around her in a comforting hug. "Don't worry, we'll figure something out." He said. A chuckle sounded from the other green caravan, and a dark shadow moved to reveal a boy, not much older than they were. "What'd you do to piss off the old woman?" He asked with a grin, stubbing out a cigarette under his boot. He was tall-at least two feet taller than Aiden, and skinny.

He had olive skin, like Lavinia with long wavy black hair, it came down to his shoulders making him look like a Gothic pirate from his skull t-shirt and black ripped jeans. "None of your business," Aiden said, frowning at him with distrust. "Chill out, I was only asking what you said, after all gotta look out for my gran," he aimed a wink towards Isabelle who was also frowning, but looking the less hostile of the two. "Your gran?" Aiden asked which earned him another one of those cheeky grins. "Yeah, crazy old bat that she is, she's still family, and you gotta look out for family haven't you?" He said he seemed friendly enough but Aiden didn't trust anyone until he had gotten to know them better, and he didn't plan for them to stick around long enough to be pals. The news that this was Lavinia's grandson however had a plan forming in his mind.

"The name's Cam." he held out his hand and Aiden took it, shaking briefly. "I'm Aiden, this is Isabelle." he introduced them, Isabelle gave a shy wave. "What's the matter, cat got your tongue?" Cam said to Isabelle with a wink. Aiden scowled and said "she *can't* talk, it's part of why we're here," Aiden explained. "We came for help, but it looks like she's not going to help us, considering she just threw us out," Aiden said shrugging, Isabelle shot him a look, what was he doing? She thought, the less people knew about this the better. The boy looked thoughtful, "did you ask nicely?" he asked them "she's a little eccentric, very old school. If you let her cool off then maybe..." he began but Isabelle and Aiden shook their heads. "We don't have time to wait. A life is at stake." Aiden said, Isabelle pulled on his arm and shook her head. "If he's her grandson then he might be able to help us, think about it, Izzy. What have we got to lose?" he whispered to her, she hesitated before signing *"but can we trust him?"* and Aiden sighed "we don't really have a choice. We're running out of time."

"Well, well, you two just got very interesting..." Cam said watching their conversation. "Are you gonna tell me why you're both here or what?" he said, suggesting: "maybe I can help you." Aiden looked to Isabelle who looked as if she was thinking hard, finally she nodded. *"Tell him."* Aiden gave Cam the once over look, before saying, "do you believe in magic?" there was something about Cam that rubbed him up the wrong way, maybe it was the cocky attitude, or the way he looked at Isabelle, but now was not the time to be picky, they needed all the help they could get. "Magic? Like all that smoke and mirrors crap you see on TV?" Cam asked, grinning. "No. I mean the real stuff." Aiden said, his voice serious. Cam's eyebrows raised and he said "well then, you better come in." he gestured to the caravan he had been leaning on. He opened the door for them and nodded for them to go first.

They shared an uncertain look but went in all the same. "Home sweet home," he said, it was nowhere near as tidy as Lavinia's had been. There were piles of clothes strewn about, a full ashtray on the table. There were iron maiden posters, and Metallica, a black and white guitar stood in a corner. On the shelves there were different shaped and coloured bongs. **Clearly he liked to smoke more than just cigarettes,** Aiden thought. "Sorry it's a mess, don't get many visitors." Cam said ruefully, clearing a space for them to sit down on the booth like seats he had. "I'm not sure where to start," Aiden said, feeling kind of unnerved by the surroundings. He didn't think somehow that this was the person to help after all. Cam leaned forwards, his elbows on the table, he steepled his hands and rested his chin on them, giving them his undivided attention. "Start from the beginning." Cam said looking from Aiden to Isabelle who both seemed unsure. "Well...have you ever heard of curses?" Aiden began.

****

Cam took it all surprisingly well, he listened without interrupting and stayed surprisingly calm as Isabelle showed him the scars. "So it's a bloodline curse you say?" he asked, his eyes tracing the pink puckered lines on Isabelle's arm with the tip of his finger, making goosebumps raise on her arm, he seemed fascinated with them. "Say something now, just so I can be sure you're not just having me on," Cam said and Isabelle looked at him in shock. "What the hell!" Aiden said "you want her to put her life at risk just so she can prove to you we're telling the truth? No way man!" he was fuming, "come on, Izzy, we can find someone else to help," he stood to leave, but Cam held his hands up.

"Hold on a sec, I didn't mean to upset you guys," he said "It's just I have to be sure you're not scammers. Bad for business." he looked at them ruefully. "All friends again?" he asked, Isabelle put her hand on Aiden's arm and after they shared a look Aiden sat back down again, although begrudgingly. "She's not going to say anything to you at all, until you agree to help us." Aiden said, and Cam pursed his lips

. "If Gran says there's a cure, then I could maybe persuade her to give it to me," he said "but it'll cost ya," back was the cocky grin. "How much?" Aiden said as Isabelle looked at them both disbelievingly. "How about…£800?" Cam said, "sounds fair enough to me," Aiden shook his head at the Goth, "no way, we're school kids, where'd you think we'd get money like that?" he asked. "Ok then, what about £500?" Cam suggested and Aiden snorted. Isabelle scowled. *"My father's dying, you'd think he would cut us some slack,"* she signed to Aiden who shrugged. "What's she saying?" Cam asked, he continued to watch Isabelle like she was a specimen under a telescope. "She's wondering why you're trying to rip us off when her father is lying in a coma dying." Aiden said and Cam finally turned his gaze to Aiden. "A man's gotta earn a living, both my parents are dead. Car crash," he said, "So don't go thinking I don't know what it's like." Isabelle felt guilty then, after all she had her mum, and her dad wasn't dead, yet.

Seeing her expression Cam grinned "don't go all feeling sorry for me, I still had gran, and Aunt Sophie. She's the one who left me this caravan, after she went. Cancer. Can't complain, at least I got a roof over my head." he looked around himself before looking at his two new guests. "Bet one of you two live in one of those big houses, bet your parents have a job...lots of money to buy lots of stuff...surely you couldn't spare at least £200?" he asked. Isabelle and Aiden looked at each other, between them they had about £400, if they gave him some of the money, and it turned out he couldn't help, they could end up stranded here. He'd have to call his parents, and he wasn't ready to face them just yet.

He sighed and said, "you can have the £200, but you'll have to help us first." he said. Cam raised an eyebrow at them, "how bout, £100 now and then you can give me the other £100 after it's done?" he put to them, Aiden looked to Isabelle who shrugged. "Ok fine, but we want to help. That way we'll be in the loop and you can't run off with our money," Aiden said, grinning Cam held out his hand "shake on it?" he said. Aiden took his offered hand and shook. "Deal." he said.

\*\*\*\*

The next couple of days went rather slowly, after the agreement, Cam had been true to his word and had gone to his Gran. "She's still being rather hazy about it, she basically told me to stay out of it. That no good will come of helping you two," Cam said one day, while they looked through his aunt's old books. "So basically, we're screwed?" Aiden asked, but Cam just gave a sly smile "no, actually I'd say we're on the right track. It's only a matter of time before we find something," he said.

In the middle of all the half-eaten snacks and cans of sugary pop were old leather tomes and handwritten ledgers. It was getting rather late and they were just about ready to call it a day. "I need some fresh air, it's so stuffy in here," Aiden said "you coming?" he asked Isabelle, she just shook her head "ok, see you in a min, call me if you need me," he said giving Cam a pointed look, he still didn't like him or trust him. She was reading a passage in one of the tomes, about healing warts using

**half a potato:** *'Cut a potato in half and rub the wart firmly with the potato half, making sure that the skin becomes saturated with raw potato juice. Repeat morning and night for two weeks to start seeing results. Soak a cotton wool ball in apple cider vinegar and apply directly to the wart...'*

Shaking her head Isabelle turned a page. "He doesn't like me much, your boyfriend," Cam said, Isabelle shrugged after all they weren't here to make friends. "Ah well...you win some you lose some, eh?" he said again, she knew what he was doing, he was trying to get her to talk. "Surely just one word wouldn't hurt you?" he said, "come on, I'm dying to find out what your voice sounds like," he grinned at her. He had a swagger about him that suggested his confidence in his appearance. She looked him up and down, sure he was good looking in an Eboy kind of way, he would be the kind of guy who was right at home on a Tick Tock channel. But he definitely knew it, and she didn't like that kind of guy. His hazel green eyes laughed at her, daring her to talk but she just shook her head at him.

"I don't mean to be so pushy; I don't get a lot of girls coming round to my place." he said, she raised an eyebrow at him. **I don't think that's all very believable** she thought. As if reading her mind, he said "it's true, not a lot of girls are into gypsy's. Sure they like my bad boy looks but when it comes down to it they want stability and I just can't give them that, we move around too much for that," he said a little bitterly. She felt sorry for him, it must have been hard losing your parent's and having no stability in his young life. "Don't feel bad for me. I'm doing ok," he said and yet again she felt strange, like he had read her mind. "Your face is pretty much an open book; your expressions aren't that hard to read." he said to her. "Don't worry, Izz, we'll get to the bottom of this and save your father." he put a reassuring hand on her shoulder. She signed thank you at him, an easy sign to understand and he grinned.

"Don't worry about it." he said, even if he was getting paid to help, Isabelle was grateful all the same. "I think it's time we head off," Aiden said coming back into the caravan. Cam jerked and pulled his hand away, looking guilty, although there wasn't anything to look guilty for, he hadn't been trying anything, had he? Isabelle thought. Aiden looked at them suspiciously before holding out a hand to her. "Coming?" he said, and Isabelle took his hand. "See ya later," Cam said to them, waving as they walked away, Isabelle raised her hand and briefly waved back. Aiden scowled and Isabelle raised an eyebrow at him. "I don't like the way he looks at you." he said, turning to give him a hard stare. Isabelle smacked his shoulder, he had no reason to feel jealous, he was helping them. *"We need to keep him on our side,"* Isabelle signed, *"please, don't do anything to make him mad. We need him, my father needs him,"* Aiden sighed at her and his shoulders slumped. "I know," he said "I'm sorry, but it doesn't mean I have to like him..." he turned to look at Cam one last time, catching the smug smile on his face. **No,** Aiden thought, **I don't like him at all...**

\*\*\*\*

Isabelle had given Cam her number, so she wasn't surprised when he called. "Hey Izzy, sup?" he said "can you guys come back to the caravan? I think I'm gonna need help with all these books. Is Aiden there?" he asked. Isabelle passed over the phone. "Hullo?" Aiden asked sleepily, "hey bud, its me." Cam's voice said from the other line. "Hey man, what's up?" Aiden asked him warily, he still didn't know what to make of him. "I was just saying to your girl, its gonna take some time going through all these books, can you come over?" He asked and Aiden thought for a while. "It's getting late, can't it wait?" He asked, they were going to go out in a while and get some food. "I suppose? Can Izzy's dad wait much longer?" Cam asked and Aiden sighed. "Sure, we'll be over, we just need to grab some food first." Aiden said scratching at the back of his head. "Sure, sure...hey, if you're going to Mackey D's can you bring me two big macs and some fries? I got the munchies," Cam asked brightly. "Yeah, ok that's fine." Aiden said shaking his head. "Stock up on coffee too as this could take a long time." Cam said. After Aiden clicked the button to end the call, he slumped back on the bed with a groan. Isabelle tapped him and he looked up, *"what's wrong?"* She asked and he rubbed at his eyes. "He wants us to help him sort through his books. Says it'll be a late night." He looked tired and Isabelle felt guilty that she had dragged him into her drama. *"Sorry."* She signed and he smiled at her, "don't be. I'd do anything for you, you know that." He said and he meant it. He was beginning to fall for her and although the relationship was new, he was willing to walk through fire if it meant she would be safe. If putting up with that asshole for a few hours helped Izzy and her dad then he could do it.

They got changed quickly and then took a trip to McDonald's. They ate theirs on the tram down to Cam. It wasn't the best food but it was yummy and warm, so it filled a need. *"Cams food will be cold by the time we get there,"* Isabelle signed, Aiden shrugged, the boy had asked for them so he can take them how it is. Or he could zap them in the microwave...if he had one. After a couple of knocks, Cam answered the door to the caravan. "Sup?" He asked, running his hand through his messy hair, it was sticking up in places like an unkempt mop. "Hey, here's your big macs," Aiden said handing over the slightly soggy brown paper bag with the food. "You're the best!" Cam said pulling out a wrapped-up burger and taking a bite before they had even sat down. "Hmm..." he said appreciatively, closing his eyes in bliss. It seemed he didn't care if it was cold or not. "Much better," Cam said.

"Come sit down, help yourself a pile," he gestured in front of him and then sat down himself. "I've been translating these here. But this pile here is already in English so you can start there. Anything that's useless, just chuck on the floor. I'll sort it later." He said and they began to work. The whole caravan stunk of cigarettes, dust and something else, Weed. Aiden checked Cams eyes and saw that they were red and glazed. Aiden curled his nose and shook his head. After a few hours of reading, Aiden said "I need the bathroom, where do you usually go?" Cam grinned "well...there's either the trusty travel potty-" he pointed to a bucket in the corner "or the public toilets over there in the park. Your choice," Aiden blushed when he looked over at Isabelle and mumbled: "...be right back," to her before he left the caravan.

"He your boyfriend or something?" Cam asked Isabelle, she shrugged at him and carried on reading. "Sorry, I keep forgetting...you know, must be hard not talking and shit? Make things hard for you?" Again, Isabelle shrugged. "Yeah, bet it makes life difficult. Anyway, you want one?" Cam asked as he took out a rolled-up cigarette. Isabelle looked at it and shook her head. She had tried one once with Stacy, but it had burned her throat and made her puke, so she was in no hurry to try it again. "Suit yourself." Cam said, putting to his lips and lighting it. A sickening sweet smell came from the cigarette and Isabelle wrinkled her nose. "Sorry, does smell a bit, but it's the only thing that helps me sleep." He said blowing out a puff of the smoke. "Here ya go," he said opening the doors, "get some fresh air in," he said, taking Aiden's vacated seat. "Have a break you deserve it." He said to her. He gave her one of his cheeky grins, "you still in school?" He asked conversationally, and Isabelle nodded. "What are you both, 15? 16?" He asked and again she nodded. Cam sighed, shaking his head. "Must suck, being you." He said, he casually threw an arm round the back of the chair she was sitting on. She felt a sliver of unease. Up close she could appreciate how handsome he was with his square jaw and his green hazel eyes. But she couldn't help comparing him with Aiden. There was something rugged about Cam, he was good-looking in an untouchable, bad boy way with his wicked grin and cocky attitude, where Aiden's was a friendly, sweet kind of way. Cam was a heart breaker. And yet he still drew her to him, despite the fact she was falling in love with Aiden, it felt like other forces were at work here.

"You're very pretty," he said his voice soft. "Such a shame..." he reached out a finger and stroked her face. Her heart began to race, what did he want from her? Was he going to *kiss* her? Did she want him to? She didn't know if she should slap him or kiss him back if he did. It was confusing...The sweet smell of the roll up he was smoking wafted around her, clogging her throat, and making her feel funny. "Hey, it's getting late, you ready to go?" Aiden's voice called as he walked up to the caravan. Isabelle jumped as if she had been shocked and even Cam seemed flustered, moving away from her. "Izzy?" Aiden called as he poked his head in. *"I'm coming,"* she signed to him, jumping up. "Here, take these," Cam said handing over a pile of books. "Thanks," Aiden said, taking them and putting them in his rucksack. "When you've finished with them, these will need to be sorted through," he said to another pile.

"Where'd you get all these?" Aiden asked, "some are gran's, some are my aunt Sophie, but I did some asking around so be careful with them, I've got to give them back." He explained, "when do we meet again," Aiden asked him. "Hmm...tomorrow if that's ok?" Cam suggested, scratching at the stubble on his chin. "Could you maybe come to us? We're running low on cash and if you want that £200 you gotta help us figure this out fast." Aiden said, it was expensive on the train as well as cabs. "Sure, I can use the motorbike." Cam said, at the mention of motor bike Aiden's eyes lit up.

"You have a motorbike? What kind?" He asked, Cam grinned and stood up, pulling aside the curtain that served as a room divider to the bedroom revealing a small cot bed with the black motorbike tucked up the side of the room. Isabelle blushed and looked away, there on the walls he had taped pictures of topless girls. Aiden only had eyes for the motorbike. "It's just a Honda, I'm saving for a Harley, but she's still fast." Cam said, "I keep begging my dad for one, but he wants me to have a car. How fast does she go?" Aiden said glumly. Isabelle shook her head, boys, and their toys. She let them talk about the bike for a while before tapping him and pointing to her watch. "Oh yeah, we best be off. See you," Aiden giving the bike one last look of longing before leaving the caravan. Cam waved to them before shutting the doors. Isabelle looked over at Aiden. "What?" He asked, seeming in a better mood. Isabelle shook her head at him and gave him a playful push. He was such a *boy*. He threw an arm around her and laughed as they walked to the station, ignoring the confused feelings Isabelle had had moments before, pushing them from her mind. Aiden was the one she wanted.

# CHAPTER 10. SMOKE AND ASHES

The old woman was waiting for him. She sat in her plump pink chair, knitting. Dressed in her white nightgown with a pink crochet shawl wrapped around his shoulders, on her lap was the magic spell book. Her white wispy hair was down and curled around her face which made her seem younger somehow. She looked up from her hands to see him standing in front of her, dressed all in black, the hood of his hoodie pulled low over his face so as not to be recognised. But she knew exactly who he was, and why he was here-he should have known by now that the woman's psychic gifts were too strong to be fooled.

"I've been waiting for you," she said, her thick accent washing over him and making him shiver. "I see you have a lot of questions." she said, though the intruder kept quiet. He had not expected her to be awake and waiting for him, this complicated things. He meant to come in and steal the book, leaving the old crone asleep in her bed and none the wiser for his crime. He didn't answer her, he was **angry** with her! She should have just let him take the book. "I didn't mean to lie to you...this book. It's an **evil** thing. You don't want it; all it does is cause pain and destruction." she shuddered. "It was given to me to keep safe, but never to use. Never again..." she said looking at him pleadingly. An anger was building inside of him, how could she think to keep it from him? It was his book. Its secrets belonged to him. "Give it to me, old woman, and no one gets hurt," he said, his voice gruff and muffled by the mask he wore, he held up a penknife as he warned her. She just gave him a sad look, "I am sorry…" she said, "but I cannot let you have it," she said. The anger inside of him flared up, his insides were burning with the heat of it. "Where is the book!? Give. It. To. Me!" He demanded, she continued to look at him with those sad eyes. "It is hidden." she said. In a rage, he raised his hand and with a slashing movement, the knife in his hand whistled through the air, slicing.

There was a spray of blood, and the old woman gasped, her eyes wide with surprise and terror. *She didn't see that coming*…he thought. He pried the book out of her dying hands as she continued to stare unbelieving at him, or maybe she did know, but she refused to believe he could ever be so cruel, he corrected himself. He had slit her throat, but the old woman still refused to die, she held her hands to the wound and gasped shallow breaths. No matter…it could be put right, the intruder thought.

He walked away to the door with the book, thinking hard. If someone found her here like this then it would be obvious this was murder…he thought hard, he looked about the room them gasped, the answer was obvious, as he looked at the hundreds of candles flickering dimly. If there was a fire then no one would look too closely into this, it would be a terrible accident, people were always telling her to get electric lighting, candles were dangerous...he let out a terrible laugh, and looked over at Lavinia Bosswell. He reached over and picking up the closest candle he raised it to light the end of one of the curtains. It ignited rather quickly and began to travel upwards, he watched for a moment longer, mesmerised by the destructive nature of it. When he was satisfied, he left the caravan, now aflame. He wasn't too far away when he heard the first of the screaming, obviously the other travelers had now seen the flames. But it would be too late, much too late. A hateful grin stole over his face as he kept walking.

****

Aiden and Isabelle had an early breakfast as they had agreed to meet Cam back at the caravan site. They didn't notice anything wrong until they came upon the car park. There were police cars, fire trucks and an ambulance. Looking at each other fearfully, they picked up their pace. The air was thick with the smell of smoke, "oh no!" Aiden said, and after grabbing Isabelle's hand, he tugged her after him as he jogged. There was a crowd of people, being held back by the police, a few were weeping but most looked shocked. "Excuse me," Aiden managed to push a path through to see what had happened. Isabelle gasped and tears sprung to her eyes. The once grand red caravan was a smoldering mess. Small wisps of black smoke still rose in curls from the charred wood, though it was clear it had not been on fire for a while. Aiden and Isabelle looked at the wreck in fear and sadness, where was Lavinia? "...I tried to call out to her, officer but the fire had gone too far for me to get in there," a soot covered man said to a uniformed policeman, who seemed to be taking notes. "We tried to put out the fire ourselves, but we weren't enough," he carried on, and it dawned on Aiden. Lavinia was dead. Before he could say anything to Isabelle however, two officers in white suits and face's masks carried out a body bag. Isabelle gasped and tucked her head into his shoulder, he held onto her but continued to search around-

"Cam!" He shouted, spotting the boy standing near to the wreck watching as they took his gran away. He didn't seem to hear, so Aiden edged forwards, a police officer pushed him back. "Get back, this is a police investigation," he barked angrily, it seemed that the gaggle of onlookers was agitating the officer. "That's our friend, over there!" Aiden pointed to Cam, it was a lie and yet they needed to know what had happened. "I don't bloody care if it were your uncle over there, until we know what happened this is a murder zone so get back!" He griped at them. "We just want to know if he's ok," Aiden said though the policeman ignored them. Aiden shouted Cam again and he spotted them. He said something to an offer and jogged over to them. "What happened?" Aiden asked, looking at the destruction around them. "There's been a fire, my-my gran was still inside I tried to get in, but the fire was out of control." Cam raised his bandaged hands. "Oh god!" Aiden said his face pale, Isabelle had her hands over her mouth and was crying. "We're so sorry," Aiden said, Cam made the corner of his mouth lift, "the smoke would have gotten her first, they said. At least she wouldn't have felt..." his face puckered, and he began to weep. Isabelle rushed forwards and wrapped her arms around him. Aiden felt a twinge of jealousy before he clamped down on it. His grandmother is dead, no need to be a jerk, she's just comforting him...he scolded himself. Pulling back, Cam wiped his eyes.

"They want me to go back with them to the hospital, get my hands seen to properly." He said, "then the police want an interview...I'm sorry I'm not going to be much help to you for a while," he said. Aiden patted him on the back saying, "we understand, I'm sorry for your loss." and Isabelle nodded. Cam went back to the ambulance, and Aiden put his arm around Isabelle's shoulder. "Come on, there's nothing we can do," they walked away from the grisly scene. *"It's awful,"* Isabelle signed, *"I wonder how it happened,"* she couldn't believe that not long after they had spoken to her, Lavinia had died. This couldn't be a coincidence, could it? "Probably one of those candles fell over and set fire to the place," Aiden said "I thought it looked dangerous when I saw them all yesterday. She should have got electricity fitted." He shook his head, deep in thought. *"Poor Cam,"* Isabelle signed, "yeah...poor Cam," Aiden agreed, *"to first lose your parents then your gran...he must be devastated."* Isabelle continued. "Yeah...it's not something you can just get over." Aiden said, thinking of his sister. "Come on, let's get out of here," he steered Isabelle around and they started walking.

\*\*\*\*

The gloomy grey interior of the hotel had suited their gloomy mood. It took Cam 3 days to contact them again (which didn't help Isabelle's anxiety) and it was to tell them to meet him in the hotel lobby. She was scared for her father and worried about her mother. She was worried about Aiden's parents and how angry they would be when he got back home. Would they be banned from seeing each other outside of school? Aiden kept telling her it would all work out ok, but it didn't stop her worrying. They agreed to keep their phones switched off in case the police had been involved and were trying to track them, and only use them to send texts to their families saying they were ok. Her mother had sent her hundreds of texts, telling her to come home, that she knew what she was doing and to be careful not to make things worse. The latest text was to tell her that her father was pretty much the same. That he was still holding on in the intensive care unit, that he still wasn't breathing on his own. His outcome if they didn't get this curse broken looked pretty bleak. Which was why Cam had agreed to meet with them, despite losing his gran. Aiden knew what it was like, to lose someone dear and he still wanted to help Isabelle save her dad, so he had to admire Cam's strength and commitment to their cause.

"Over here!" A voice shouted and they turned to see Cam waving at them as he walked through the entrance. Dressed all in black again, this time with a biker's jacket, he seemed in better spirits than the last time they saw him. Tucked under his arm was a plastic shopping bag full of books. Cam Loped up to them pretty quickly, giving Isabelle a hug. *"How are you?"* She asked, Cam looked to Aiden for translation, though Aiden seemed a little put out by it. "She wants to know how you are doing," Aiden said, and Cam gave Isabelle a warm smile. "I'm doing ok, thanks. Despite what happened...I know she's in a better place now. With my parent's." He said, shrugging. His eyes were red from crying but he was trying not to show his pain. Isabelle reached up and patted his shoulder. He gave her a brave smile, grateful for her comfort.

"Do the police know what happened?" Aiden asked. "They think that she knocked over one of the candles, they're ruling it an accident..." Cam said though he seemed unsure. "But?" Aiden guessed and Cam nodded. "**But** I know gran. She's had those candles for as long as I remember, she was always careful around them. She never went to sleep without blowing them out first." He said, "but I guess she was getting on in years and her eyesight *was* failing her. It could have been an accident." Cam said shrugging. "But you don't think it was," Aiden said with a bit of skepticism leaking into his voice, after all he had seen all the candles and the old woman had seemed frail. Cam just shrugged. "Ok. Let's just get this over with, after all...I've got a funeral to plan." he said starting to walk towards the elevators, Aiden looked to Isabelle who just shrugged. They entered the elevators together, and Aiden punched in the number of the floor they were on.

\*\*\*\*

Cam looked around him at the hotel room, looking out of place in his dark leather. "Pretty nice set up you got here," he said, and Isabelle blushed, thinking that it was Aiden's parents and her own that had paid for it. "It's ok I guess," Aiden said, brushing the comment off. Despite the boy's grandma being dead, there was still something about him that Aiden didn't like. He was always looking at Isabelle with a hungry, predatory look which put Aiden's hackles up. She was **his** girlfriend. "Right, first things first, those books we've been looking over, my Aunts. I finished translating them and they're no good. But some of my grandma's books were saved." he plonked himself onto the bed. Opening the bag, he had bought with him he placed the leather book down. One was quite big and old looking, its edges were burnt and a little worse for wear. "I think these are more likely to be helpful." he said "they look old enough and from what I managed to translate last night, this one-" he held up the old, burnt book "has some serious curse work in it. It might be our guy." he said. Isabelle looked at the book and shivered.

It had a pentagram on it with some Romanian words in gold. "So, what do you need us for?" Aiden asked, frowning. "These other books are in English, I haven't bothered with them yet, but it would be stupid to count them out completely. I need you two to look through them." he said handing over the other books. They each picked one up and went over to the table. They had their notepads and pens already there, from their earlier internet search, it hadn't been going too well but Aiden still thought it would help to have a search anyway. They had jotted down anything they thought might be useful. Cam had already made himself at home, he had taken his shoes off and was lying on the bed, on his stomach, with his legs crossed and sticking up in the air a little. Aiden tried to ignore how much it irritated him to see the lad on the bed like he owned the place.

After a few hours of searching, Isabelle stretched and yawned. *"Nothing in here."* she signed, it had been a small book, but it mainly contained cures for hiccups, ointments for cuts and bruises. Nothing about curse breaking. She picked up another book, sighing. It was quite boring reading after a while. Aiden screwed up his face and quickly turned the page, "ugh!" he said, "that's nasty," he shuddered, *"what?"* Isabelle asked and craned her head to see what had disgusted him. "Just a list of ingredients for a poultice to cure a toenail fungal infection..." he said, "there was a gross looking drawing..." he shuddered again. Isabelle screwed up her own face thinking 'ew...' she definitely didn't want to see that.

She looked over to Cam, his face was that of deep concentration, he scratched at the stubble on his chin with his pen, eyes narrowed. He *was* quite handsome, in a cheeky, bad boy way. She could imagine he would have to beat the girls away, with that attitude he had, girls liked a bad boy. He wasn't Aiden though, and she loved everything about him. She felt aspirated that Aiden was jealous, but at least it showed that he cared enough about her to be jealous of any other guy showing her attention, even if she suspected that Cam was doing it on purpose to get a rise out of Aiden. Cam scribbled something down then turned the page. "Any luck?" Aiden asked Cam, as he noticed Isabelle looking over at the older boy. Cam looked up and pursed his lips, "nah, not yet. But it's interesting reading, I can see why my gran kept this book away from me," he said, holding up a page, showing handwritten pages with gruesome drawings. "If the cure is going to be somewhere, it'll be in here." he said. "What do we do once we have the cure?" Aiden asked, "your grandmothers dead, so who is going to do the magic?" He felt that it needed addressing, though by the glare sent his way from Isabelle he thought he could have been a little bit more tactful, even so they were running out of time.   "I'll do it." Cam said, "after all, it's in my family, how hard can it be?" he shrugged. "Have you ever used magic before?" Aiden asked and again Cam shrugged. "I've helped my gran with stuff before, she's done magic to help cure cancer, things like that..." he said, and Isabelle looked at him interested. "Has she ever cured anyone of cancer before?" she asked, and Aiden was forced to translate. "I'm not sure, they never came back to say if it helped." he said, "I hope so..." he looked saddened by this.

"So, you think you can do the spell, Cure Isabelle yourself?" Aiden asked, doubt written all over his face. "Yeah, that's if we actually find the spell." Cam said, shrugging. Isabelle gave him a smile, he was more invested in this than he made out he was, *"I have every faith you will,"* she signed. Aiden managed to look hurt at this but said "we know you'll find it. Izzy believes in you," he translated, Cam gave her a cheeky smile "thanks, Izzy. I best be off now if I don't want a ticket." He stood and started gathering up some of the Romanian books, "I'll carry on with this when I get home. I'll give you a call if- no when I find something." He said, they nodded and agreed with him before saying their goodbyes.

****

As Cam walked down the corridor, a voice called out to him and he turned to see Aiden hurrying after him. "Sup?" Cam asked as Aiden slowed down to a stop in front of him. "Look, I appreciate all that you're doing for Izzy, you've gone way beyond for us, I just..." he seemed as if he was struggling to say the words he wanted to, Cam knew exactly why he was here, and he could have helped him out but he liked to see the kid squirm. "I just feel uncomfortable with you flirting with her." Aiden said blushing a little with an embarrassed smile, Cam just raised an eyebrow and pursed his lips-mainly to stop from laughing at the boy, but also to rile him up further. "I wasn't aware I was," Cam said shrugging, ignoring the no smoking he took out a cigarette from his jacket, he put it in his mouth but didn't light it. Aiden seemed flustered at the comment but carried on.

"I don't mind you all being friends, I just wanted to make it clear to you that Izzy and I are in a relationship, as in boyfriend and girlfriend. So, you won't, you know...try anything with her." Aiden said, his jaw set. "Looks to me like you've got a case of the of the green-eyed monster," Cam said, smirking. "That's not-I'm trying to look out for her, not being able to talk it takes it out of her, she can't stick up for herself, it makes her uncomfortable..." Aiden defended himself, and Cam smiled. That's what Cam had been waiting for, that spark of flames in his eyes, the tightening of the fists, he liked making people angry it was a thrill all on its own, knowing that at any moment they could fight...the pain of being punched, the adrenaline...he was always seeking the next thrill. It was one of the reasons he bought the bike, his aunts old horse Chester was slowing down so it wasn't fun anymore, but he still needed the beast to move with the other caravans. Now he had his grans horse Gabriella, too, things might be more interesting next time they moved on. For now, though, he supposed he better defuse the situation, it had been a long time since he had a project this good, he was itching to do some real magic of his own.

"She says that I made her feel uncomfortable?" Cam asked interested, and Aiden hesitated. "Not exactly, but then she doesn't like conflict." he said and Cam felt a vindictive stab of triumph, he didn't fancy Isabelle, sure she was pretty but she was a little on the plain side despite the curse, a little too goodie-goodie for his taste. He liked his women with a little more fire, but this was fun. Testing people's relationships was as entertaining to him as someone else watching a football match. Sticking his cigarette behind his ear he said, "do you think it would have been best to ask her first before having it out with me? Maybe you should trust her to do the right thing, after all she's *your* girlfriend, am I right?" Cam asked and Aiden could see the conversation was being turned against him, he could argue till the sun came down, but Aiden knew they needed him. Shoulders slumping, Aiden said "I guess..."

Cam grinned at this then said "look, I'm not after your girl. You can rest easy. I was just being myself, but if it makes you and her feel uncomfortable then I'll stop. No harm done." He smiled and held out his hand, a peace offering. Aiden, still a little mistrustfully, reached over and shook his hand. "Good. Talk to you later," Cam said cheerfully, and after a more subdued, muttered reply from Aiden, he was on his way again.

\*\*\*\*

Back in the hotel room Aiden seemed a little subdued. *"Are you ok? Did Cam say something to you?"* Isabelle asked, Aiden sighed, "I think it was more what I said." He confessed, after all what he had said made sense. He should have asked Izzy first before he went all guns blazing. But he felt protective of her, she was his first proper girlfriend and he had messed up already. *"What did you say?"* She signed, looking at him a little suspiciously. " I kind of told him to back off. From you." Aiden said blushing, *"but...why did you did that?"* She asked horrified, Aiden ducked his head. "I didn't like him flirting with you. It's ok though, it didn't offend him enough not to want to help us." He said remembering the smug smile. *"What did he say?"* Isabelle asked feeling half exasperated, half flattered that Aiden was 'defending his girlfriend'. Aiden sighed again, running a hand through his hair. "He basically told me off, said before I run my mouth, I should talk to you about it." He said, not used to being told he was wrong about something. *"Maybe you should have, then I could have told you there was nothing to worry about."* Isabelle said, ignoring the guilty feeling as she remembered the other night at the caravan. "Are you mad at me?" Aiden asked, after all what he had done, it was in the same possessive category of what Josh had done, and he didn't like being tarred with the same brush as that jerk.

But there was this feeling in his gut, however irrational, telling him that something was off about Cam, something wasn't right. But if he were a bad person would he really help two strangers? Was this all some kind of jealousy thing? He was confused. Isabelle tapped him on the shoulder, bringing his attention back to her, *"I'm not mad at you. I just wish you'd have talked to me about it. Next time, just tell me how your feeling, ok?"* Isabelle signed to him. "I promise." Aiden said smiling, no longer distracted. She leaned over and kissed his lips. After that they *were* both distracted for a while. They ended up having a break from research, they ordered food from room service, then watched some TV. They even fell asleep for a little while.

The phone ringing woke them up with a start. Aiden fumbled his hand on the bedside cabinet and picked it up. "Hello?" He asked groggily. "I got it!" Said an excited voice from the other side of the phone, "what?" Aiden asked, "the cure! I found it!" Cam said and after a moment's pause an excited feeling filled his own belly, "for real?" Aiden asked holding the phone tighter in his grasp, "Yeah, I'm positive," Cam said. After another pause Aiden said "can you do it? Can you cure Izzy with it?" He asked hope thick in his voice, "I *think* so. I've never really done any spells, just helped gran with them but we have to try, don't we? For Izzy's dad?" Cam said. Aiden made a noise in agreement. "How do we do this?" Aiden asked, there was a noise on the other side of the phone, like a bag rustling or something. "Meet me at Highgate Cemetery, after closing hours." Cam said and after frowning at the location Aiden asked: "When?" There was another crackle from the other end then Cam replied: "Tonight."

# CHAPTER 11. HIGHGATE CEMETERY CATACOMBS

"Are you sure about this?" Aiden asked looking around them, feeling kind of shifty as Cam picked at the locks with some tools he had bought with him. "Stop being such a pussy! Like I said it's closed and there's stuff here that I'll need for the spell to work." Cam said and Aiden frowned. "I still don't feel good about breaking into a cemetery. It seems disrespectful, not to mention it's illegal..." he said. Isabelle nodded in agreement, feeling conflicted and a little afraid. Goosebumps rose on her arms at the thought of all those dead bodies. She hoped to not have to see any of them. Cam looked back and gave a wickedly cheeky smile and said "I thought you wanted a cure, but if you're having second thoughts...you could just wait here, Izzy and I can do it without you," he said and Aiden's jaw clenched. "I'm coming," he said, everything about Cam set his teeth on edge, he was so arrogant! Plus he didn't trust him when he said earlier that he wasn't interested in Izzy, he hated the way he looked at her, almost predatory. "Well then...let's get a move on," Cam said, swinging the gate open. Isabelle and Aiden gave each other apprehensive looks, this did not feel right...also, why the catacombs? It seemed like a weird place to conduct a spell, considering they needed to be quiet about this, why somewhere so public? Even after hours? He didn't trust Cam, with his cocky grin and his overconfident swagger. He was *way* too happy to go along with this plan of breaking the curse. "Tell me again why it has to be here?" Aiden asked and Cam sighed swinging around to face him. "Look, I know you don't trust me and that's fine. But I'm the only hope she has. Just *try* to trust me on this one, Ok? It has to be done in a significantly magic area and this place is soaked in magical powers. My gran brought her customers here, sometimes she would let me watch and even join in. I'm telling you; this is the place." he said and after a sigh Aiden nodded.

They walked in silence for a while, the shadows of the headstones flickering in the light from the lampposts. It was times like this, when the sun goes down and everything turns black and blue, that made Isabelle think of her youth, in a time where she had once believed that everything was real and images of boogie monsters and monsters with terrifying faces and long clawed hands would reach up and pull her off her bed, to be dragged to a horrifying world that lived under her bed. She had grown up a lot since then but every now and then, like tonight she couldn't be so sure that they didn't exist. At least the thought that someone sinister, someone evil, might be lurking in the shadows waiting to strike.

Aiden noticed her shiver and wrapped an arm round her. She looked up with a grateful smile which he returned warmly. Everything about him was warm, safe. "Do you want a tour?" Cam asked grinning, "What? Why would we want a tour of a cemetery?" Aiden asked, feeling creeped out by the old crumbling stones and statues. Why did people think huge statues of angels were a good idea? They reminded him of that doctor who episode with the weeping angels...creepy. "It's a pretty famous area, people come from all over to have a tour here. For example: did you know that 850 notable people are buried here including 18 Royal Academics, 6 Lord Mayors of London and 48 Fellows of the Royal Society. *Henry Moore* the painter is buried here." Cam said, Aiden shook his head "sounds like you've taken the tour yourself," he muttered under his breath, out loud he said "I still don't get why anyone would find a cemetery a good place to spend a fun day activity on," Isabelle nodded with him and snuggled further into his side. "It's history," Cam said. They passed the chapel then carried on past the Lodge of the superintendent,

They ascended a flight of broad stone steps which lead up-as Cam informed them-towards the higher and more distant parts of the grounds. They made their way in further, passing decades old tombs and the dense woodland which was tough to navigate. They started to go up hill for a while. "How much further?" Aiden asked as they struggled to match Cams pace. "Not far," Cam called back. The roads had started to gradually descend again when the first view of the Catacombs came into sight. "This is called the Egyptian Avenue, the catacombs are just through here," Cam said. "Wow!" Aiden said softly, it was magnificent! Like a movie set. The focal point of the entrance was the huge Egyptian pillars and the obelisks that rose up on each side of the arch, with its heavy cornice and carved winged serpent and other Oriental ornaments it was a sight to behold. The huge fronts and greenery surrounding the pillars made her feel as if they were in a jungle. *"It's beautiful,"* she signed to Aiden, who nodded. They followed Cam through the arch under a long tunnel, and out into the side. There was a rounded structure down a set of stairs that housed the catacombs. "Hey, wasn't this in that Fantastic beasts Movie?" Aiden said, perking up at the familiar Gothic structures. "See...it's famous, nothing to be scared of," Cam said. Isabelle looked up at the look of awe Aiden was giving the place and smiled a little, Aiden loved movies. In the middle on the raised ground was a huge Cedar tree.

"The Cedar of Lebanon," Cam pointed it out, "come on," he said, and he started off with a long-legged stride down the stairs into the Avenue (the entrance of the catacombs). There were numerous square apartments, lined with stone, on each side of the avenue; these monuments when peeked inside were furnished with stone shelves, rising one above the other on three sides, capable of containing at least twelve coffins, in addition to those which could be placed upon the floor. The doors of the monuments were made of cast iron; Each of the doors had a weird sort of carving of an inverted torch upon them. There were 16 vaults in total. There was a small walkway leading to an arched room, with more coffins with a heavily padlocked Gate. It had a high ceiling, tall walls with shelves. "This will do just nicely," Cam said taking his backpack off his shoulder and opening it to pull out a pair of bolt cutters.

"Woah! No way, we've already broken and entered, now you're just going to add damage of property to the mix!" Aiden said, holding up his hands as if to be ready to pull the bolt cutters away from Cam. "Relax, they'll replace it, plus this rooms big enough to cast the spell." He said, putting open the cutters against the rusted chain. It broke with a loud snap before Aiden could say anything else. They reluctantly followed Cam inside the tomb, wincing at the loud shriek of metal on stone as the gate was opened. He placed the bolt cutters and his backpack on a shelf them rummaged around until he pulled out an old leather book, and some chalk. "I'm going to draw a pentagram on the ground, can you two light us some candles? They're in the bag." He asked and after sharing a look, they both went over to pull out the candle pillars, and after some rummaging, a neon green lighter.

After the candles were lit, and the chalk pentagram drawn he gestured for Isabelle to stand in the center. "As you're the one we're trying to cure, you need to be inside the pentagram, so its magic can help you." He said, "but aren't pentagrams you know...Evil?" Aiden asked and

Cam scoffed. "Magic is neither good nor evil, it's the intention of the magic user who shapes it to their own will. Pentagrams are used to protect us from evil. Even with demon summoning the pentagram traps the demon to stop it from hurting anyone. It's a good symbol to use." He explained, Aiden nodded. Cam bent over, picked up the book and opened it. "This is it...are you ready?" Cam asked Isabelle, she took in a deep shaky breath but nodded. She was nervous but also excited that she was saving her father, ending the curse that had troubled her family all these years...she was more than ready. "Good. Let's get this thing started." He grinned.

Cam cleared his throat and began chanting:

*"Apa, pământ, foc, aer,*

*Acest spațiu nu îl vom mai împărtăși,*

*Ochi care nu se vor mai vedea..."*

A small wind had started to pick up and swirled around the tomb, cam carried on chanting: *"Spiritul care nu mai este liber, ia de la tine acea lumină interioară..."* The wind picked up the more he chanted, his voice becoming more and more desperate. *"Luați-vă simțurile, sunetul și vederea!"* He finished the incantation and the air still swirled around them, picking up in huge gusts, whipping through their hair and clothes, making it impossible for them to move. "Er...Cam? I don't think it's working..." Aiden shouted over the howl of the storm, looking at

Isabelle's frightened face. "Are you sure this is the right spell?" he asked again, not sure if the other boy had heard him and Cam finally turned his gaze over to them. "You're right, this *isn't* working..." he said matter of fact, and Aiden frowned at him. "What?" he asked confused, and then, way too quick for Aiden to react, Cam swung a fist back and hit him squarely in the head with the torch, knocking him out cold.

# CHAPTER 12. I'M THE BAD GUY...

"Aiden! Cam <u>No</u>!" Isabelle shouted out loud as Aiden crumpled to the floor, a wet trickle of blood ran from the cut on Aiden's forehead. "What are you doing!" she exclaimed, feeling her words etch into her skin as she screamed them. She tried to run to Aiden, but Cam raised an arm and a huge gust of wind whooshed around her, trapping her. She couldn't move at all, she was stuck inside the pentagram!   "You're so stupid! You think I didn't know what you were doing?! Coming here, looking for a cure," he said to her, mocking. She frowned "what are you talking about, Cam, stop this!" she pleaded, eyes only for Aiden. "You came here looking for the cure! But what if the cure was the cure for you but meant the opposite for me? What if it means murder?!" he shouted at her.

"But-I don't understand! What do you mean? I'd never Murder anyone! I never even wanted to hurt anyone; I just want to save my dad!" she shouted back. What was he talking about? "But you did hurt someone, by just deciding to search for me, for the *cure*...but you don't know, do you? I never gave you a chance..." he muttered. **He was mad, raving mad! What was he muttering about? What did he mean?** She thought. "What are you talking about?!" she shouted out loud."*YOU THINK I'D JUST LET YOU KILL ME?!*" he shouted back at her, spittle spraying from his mouth; gone was the sexy confident boy, and in place was a wild eyed, snarling stranger- an ugly look taking over his features. *"*What*?"* She said confused and terrified out of her mind. "The only way to stop the curse is to kill me-if you have the stomach for it, you'd have to cut out my tongue, that way the I would never speak again, the curse would transfer over to my family, and you and your precious father would be free." he spat bitterly.

"But that's...that's horrible! Who would ever come up with this!?" She shouted. "This kind of magic is dark, so it stands to reason that the cure would be dark too...stupid girl. Or are you? Were you planning to kill me all along?" Cam said and Izzy shook her head at him, disbelieving. "I would *never* hurt you, why would you think that?" she asked. *"*LIAR*!"* Cam screamed at her, "you'd have killed me as soon as you found out. Think about it: you'd really choose me over your father? You and your little boyfriend over there would have done it without hesitation, you said so yourself to Nana Lavinia, you were 'desperate'," he mocked, Izzy continued to shake her head at him, he sounded like he had truly lost his mind; there was spit on the corners of his mouth, and his eyes bulged as he held the Athame out at her. "It's because of you she died, you know," he said matter of fact, and Isabelle gasped. "What?!" she said "but the police said it was a freak accident! Wait….," she narrowed her eyes at him, surely he didn't mean, did he?

"You killed her!?" she shouted horrified. Cam let out an amused laugh at this and said "yeah that's right. Once I found out she was hiding the book from me she had to go, I mean it's *my* mother's magic book, stupid bitch, she thought that to get rid of you, it might work if she got rid of the book. Big mistake! I took the book back, trapped her in her own burning caravan. Ironic, considering that's how we used to do our funerals, you know, in the old day's…" he laughed again and Isabelle shook her head at him. "So all this time when we thought you were helping us, you were trying to stop us…you only pretended to be our friend." she asked, he nodded as she came to the sudden realisation, the wind picked up a notch whirling around them, making it impossible for her to flee. "I stalled you, made you think I was on your side when really I was looking for my own spell. A spell that would allow me to be strong enough if any of your family think to come and find me ever again! No one would ever be able to touch me, I just need one more thing…" he said, and he started forwards, his intentions clear when he raised the dagger and the silver chalice. "You wouldn't!" she said horrified. "Oh yes I would...I've already called the police and when lover boy comes around they'll suspect him of the murder, that way he'll get all the blame and I'll be free to do whatever I want," Isabella glared at him, how could someone be so evil? "You won't get away with this! They'll find out the truth!" she said, hot angry tears rose to the surface in her eyes as she struggled against the invisible bonds, wishing she could run at him, maybe if she could just get the knife off him...

"It's all simple really, this spell needs a sacrifice to seal the deal, just a little bit of your blood and I'll be on my way..." he taunted "I'll make it quick." he said as if he was talking about doing the laundry or taking out the trash. "You really shouldn't have come," he said to her pityingly, his face grim but determined. He raised the knife, and Isabelle closed her eyes shut, she couldn't watch. "Don't you **dare** touch her!" said a voice. Isabelle's eyes sprung open. Aiden was awake and was standing behind Cam, he grabbed him from behind and the two boys began to struggle, the knife fell out of his hands and clattered to Isabelle's feet. The invisible bonds seemed to fall off her as he was distracted and Isabella lunged for the knife, holding it out in front of her, unsure of how to help, desperately hoping Aiden wouldn't be hurt. Cam seemed to have the upper hand, with him being taller and he managed to break free and punched Aiden on the chin, knocking him to the ground. Cam turned his wild eyes at Isabelle and ran at her. He had intended to strangle her, snap her little neck in his hands before the boy could stop him, but instead he brought about his own downfall. He had run directly into his own dagger. Isabelle felt it slam into his ribcage, there seemed to be a moment suspended in time as Isabelle locked eyes with him. She watched as they widened in surprise then change to fear as he looked down at the blade protruding from his chest; watching as the blood welled up and soaked his white tee. He looked down at it, confused, then he staggered backwards, his eyes wide.

He fell to his knees and put his hands over his chest trying to stop the blood from running away from the dagger. Aiden ran to Isabelle's side and he held her to his chest where she let out a sob. The strange, howling wind that had filled the room had stopped, leaving the crypt strangely silent after all that noise. "You...bitch.... I told you...murderer...." Cam spat, he slumped forward and rolled onto his back, Aiden approached him and glared down. "You brought this on yourself! If you'd have told us the price, we would have gone home, we're not murderers!" he wanted to add *unlike you*... but he thought that was stooping to his level. Cam coughed and blood trickled out of his mouth, "at least you've got your cure..." he gave a raspy weak chuckle then with a bout of wet coughs, he went still. "He's dead." Aiden said, looking down at his glassy eyes, feeling numb. "Oh god!" Isabelle gasped, hysteria bubbling up inside her. Aiden went over and picked up Cam's tattered old spell book. While Isabelle stood by the body, her arms wrapped around her to stop her shivers, leaving bloody handprints on her elbows. "Here," Aiden said, he pulled off his denim jacket, shook off the dirt and wrapped her in it. "Thanks..." she said. He put an arm around her shoulder and stared down at Cam. He couldn't say he was particularly sad that he was dead, he had never liked the boy, sure he had been arrogant, not to mention he had flirted with Izzy, but he would never have thought he was as psychotic as he had ended up. The sound of police sirens in the distance broke into their silent watch over the corpse.

"We need to go..." Izzy said, pulling Aiden by the arm. "But-you heard what he said- you can end this, now," Aiden said, heart hammering thinking hard about how they could do this. "There's no time!" she shouted, looking at him with terror in her eyes. "But your dad...!" he said torn between fear of getting caught and a need to help Izzy. "It's not worth it, *he's* not worth it." she said glaring at Cam's glassy eyes. She pulled on his arm again turning him around to face her. "Hurry up Aiden! Before we get arrested!" She shouted at him, looking torn, Aiden threw one last longing look at what used to be Cam, then he allowed himself to be led away from the crime scene. For that's what it was now. Police would be crawling all over this place and her one chance to break the spell would be gone. Once they were out of the crematorium they hesitated, looking down at Isabelle's top Aiden noticed that she had blood on her. "Here," he said, wrapping his jacket closer around her body, fastening it around her stomach to cover the blood. "People are going to look, it's too big for me," she said as he helped her, he put his hand over her mouth and said "Stop Izzy, stop talking! You're not cured, I don't want you dead too." He said to her and her eyes welled up with tears. "Shit, Izzy, I'm sorry, I didn't mean it like that, your dad's going to be ok. We'll figure this out." he said as he wrapped his arms around her. She pushed him back, knowing they didn't have much time left *"there will be time for crying later, we need to move,"* she signed to him, wiping angrily at her face. They snuck through the deserted graveyard, they almost made it out to the front entrance to the cemetery.

They hurried down the path, but within minutes they saw a bunch of police headed in their direction, Aiden put his arm around her shoulder-the way young couples tend to walk together, and whispered into her ear "slow down, try to act like nothing's wrong," Izabelle nodded and she slowed her pace to match his. As they got nearer the police eyed them suspiciously "evening, officers," Aiden greeted them, an easy smile on his face. Isabella gaped up at him and he gave her shoulder a gentle squeeze warning her to keep quiet, the closest officer looked from Aiden to Isabelle who was still pink and puffy eyed from crying. "Everything alright?" He asked and Aiden looked down at Isabelle. "She's just a bit upset, it was her grandmother's birthday today and we've just took some flowers down for her, haven't we love?" Aiden lied and Isabelle nodded. Still looking at them warily the officer said, "Its past closing time," he stated looking at his wristwatch and Aiden's eyes widened as he checked his own watch. "So, it it...I'm sorry officer, we didn't realize the time," he said rather convincingly, and the officer grunted. "Maybe you can help," the other officer said, "words out there's a guy with a knife out here, you two see anything suspicious?" He asked, a hand in his belt loop close to his gun.

"No, I can't say I have, sir," Aiden said, sounding surprised, giving a little believable scared look around the cemetery. "You don't think anyone is hurt, do you?" he added, sounding concerned. Ignoring his last comment, and still mistrusting but not having any evidence the officer nodded while the other with the moustache said, "Well if you remember seeing anything this is my card, don't hesitate to call us." Aiden took the card and put it in his back pocket "we will sir." He said and then faking concern he said, "I hope you catch him before any real damage is done," and the officer grunted "probably some prank callers thinking it's funny," he said. "Alright then, mind you two hurry on home. It's getting too dark to be out so late, anyone could be hiding..." the officer said, giving the shadows around him a glare.

"Mind you..." said the officer, "your both lucky you weren't locked in, the gates should have been locked by now," he said as he looked them both over again suspiciously. "They weren't locked when we came through officer...maybe the grounds keeper forgot to lock them?" Aiden suggested, the officer gave him a shrewd look, while the other nodded. "Could be...alright then. You two best be on your way, take care now." The officer said. "We will officer, thank you." Aiden said as Isabelle nodded. They tried not to hurry too fast down the path into the street but as soon as the officers were out of sight they broke into a fast walk, Aiden's arm still around her shoulders. At the train station, they slowed a little.   Once they were on the train, Isabelle looked up at Aiden, frowning at him. Was it so easy to just lie to people like that? She had killed someone, sure it was in self-defense, but someone was dead by her hands. Surely she should be in police custody!?

"Don't look at me like that," Aiden said defensively "I had to do it. Do you want us both to go to prison? You for manslaughter, me for an accessory to murder? Not to mention theft and covering up a crime," He whispered, and she shook her head. *"Theft?"* Isabelle signed "I took this," Aiden said pulling from his bag and holding up the spell book. Isabelle gasped and scowled. *"You should have left that evil thing behind; I don't want anything to do with it,"* she signed. He sighed "I'm not giving up on there being a cure, and neither are you," Aiden said, replacing the book into his bag. Isabelle scowled at him *"cam said this spell was the only way to stop the curse, it's also probably why my ancestors stopped looking for it, why my dad suddenly gave up on it."* she signed *"it's an evil spell and no good will come of it."*

They got off at their stop and carried on walking, to get back to the hotel. Isabelle shivering despite the fact she was still pressed up against Aiden's side. She felt cold all the way down to her soul, like the inside of her was filled with ice. Had she really just killed someone? Sure it was to save her own life, but she had taken someone's life away from them. It didn't matter that he was evil, he was still human and she didn't know how she could ever get over it. After walking for five minutes they met the bus stop, the one by Sainsbury's and they waited. When the bus arrived, Aiden paid and Isabelle tried not to look shifty. She could swear that the bus driver was looking at her suspiciously, she couldn't help it. She felt so...wrong. Taking the back seat they sat in silence. The only other passengers were an old man and woman-obviously a couple, a drunk who was snoozing at the front of the bus and a teenage Emo girl with her hood up and headphones in. They didn't relax until they made it back to the hotel. Aiden locked the door behind them while Isabelle slumped onto her bed, drawing up her knees and resting her chin on them. It was all over, her only chance to end the curse. Now her father was going to die and it was all her fault. No wonder her father had told her to drop it. Cam was right, she had ended up being a murderer, just by setting out on this stupid quest. She let the tears fall as Aiden paced the room, "it's just...what the hell was that git thinking...this is all so messed up..." he ran his fingers through his hair. He cursed and kicked the wardrobe. After a while he went to sit on the edge of the bed, head buried in his hands. "What do we do now?" he asked no one.

Isabelle felt tremendous guilt. She should not have dragged him into this. She scooted forwards until she was sitting next to him and put her head against his shoulder. He wrapped an arm around her, and they sat like this for a long time. *"I'm sorry,"* she signed, her hands trembling. "Don't apologize, it's not your fault he was a psycho," Aiden said, and she nodded, sniffling. Aiden stood, "I'm going to shower and change. Don't go anywhere, I'm taking the phones, just in case you feel the need to call anyone," he said, and she nodded. She didn't think she could talk at the moment, even if she wanted to. She felt so numb. She watched as he gathered his things together then shut the bathroom door, when she could hear the sound of the water running, she lay down, her head on the pillow, feeling about a hundred years old. She didn't realize she had fallen asleep until the bed dipping woke her up. "Sorry," Aiden said, as she sat up and rubbed her eyes. "You'll need to go shower," Aiden said standing, "put your dress in this bag, we need to burn anything with his blood on it," he said as he passed her a plastic bin bag.

"I've already put my clothes in there," she took the bag and looked inside it, it held his top, his jeans. She nodded feeling even more guilty that she had brought this all to him and went to shower. She took off her white dress, forever stained red and balled it up, she threw it into the bag along with her bra, and panties-she wanted no reminders, the underneath of one of her sandals was red and sticky so she threw them in, along with Aiden's denim jacket. She knotted the bag and threw it in a corner. She scrubbed at her skin till it was pink and sore, checking under her nails for blood and dirt, scrubbing her hair, until she was absolutely sure she was clean, she wanted no part of that monster on her. He had killed that poor old woman. His own grandmother! He was so evil.

After she dressed, she went back out to Aiden, who was on the phone. "She's here..." he said and held out the phone to Isabelle. She took it wordlessly and held it up to her ear. "Oh, thank goodness, I've been so very worried! You haven't been answering my calls..." her mother said,

Isabelle gripped the phone in both hands, pressing it hard to her ear, she wanted to crawl into the phone and hold her. "Look, honey, I want you to come home ok? Forget the cure, please! I just want you home, with us, safe. Your father...he would want you to be safe." her voice wobbled and Isabelle broke into silent sobs, she could tell it was very hard on her mother, with her father being so ill and with her going AWOL, but she didn't know if she could go home, not after what had happened. "Honey?" her mother asked hopefully, and Aiden took the phone off her. "Trish?" he said, and she barely heard her mother's reply, "yeah, she's ok. She's...just tired.... yeah, yeah, I'll tell her. I know. Ok. Bye." and he ended the call. He turned to Izzy and ran a hand through his hair. "You had 29 missed calls, I had to answer. Plus, we need to go home. It's not safe here." She nodded in agreement. How was she going to tell her mother that the cure was impossible? How was she going to tell her that she had killed someone?

Things had gotten so messed up, she had only wanted to save her father, now two people were dead because of her. She was a bad person. "Come on, we need to try and sleep." Aiden said, opening up the covers for her, she climbed in and he tucked them around her. He was just about to go to the sofa where he had been sleeping but Isabelle's hand shot out, grabbing his wrist. He looked down at her. *"' Stay with me? I'm scared to be alone..."*

she asked and sighing he said "ok," and got into the other side of the bed. He wrapped her in his arms, and she felt a little safer. Still didn't change what she had done. She didn't think she would sleep, but she eventually did. Though her dreams were filled with evil laughter and blood and death. When she woke in the morning Aiden was already up. He was talking on the phone and was pacing. The TV was on quietly and what the newsagent said caught her attention:

**"...police got a call, late last night that someone was seen walking around Highgate Cemetery with a knife, it has now confirmed that a young man, Camilo 'Cam' Boswell, age 20, was found inside the Highgate Cemetery Catacombs, stabbed to death.** *(*A photograph of Cam, a passport picture by the look of it, was shown on the screen.) **It is unclear of the motive, or why Mr. Boswell was even inside the Catacombs, but there has been speculations of Cult activity, as leaked photographs from the crime scene show a crude drawing of a chalk pentagram-(**a photograph crossed the right hand corner of the screen, showing cam's 5 pointed star pentagram, along with the candles and a bunch herbs)-**that was found only feet away from the body. Police urge people to give any details they may know about the murder...**

Aiden switched off the TV, Isabelle continued to stare at the blank TV, her hands over her mouth. *They were going to Prison*! She began to shake uncontrollably and sobs built up in her throat. "Hey, it's ok, Izzy, it's ok," Aiden said, rushing over to hold her. She shook her head: no, this was *not* ok. "They just said the police have no clue, we're **safe**." Aiden said and she shook her head again. *"I'm still a killer..."* she signed *"and my father is still going to die,"* she sobbed, and Aiden sighed, putting his head on top of hers. "He's the killer, not you. He would have killed you and he killed his own gran. The guy was **evil**. You only did what you had to, to survive." He said to her. Isabelle sniffled, looking up at him with tear a streaked face.

*"So, you don't think I'm a murderer?"* She signed and he pulled away from her to look her directly in the face. "You're not a murderer. You saved me! You're a hero." He said and she scoffed. *"That's not what they're saying on the news..."* she signed and Aiden shook his head. "The police don't know any of the details; they don't know what really went on. They'd give you a medal if they knew what you did." Aiden said and she shook her head pushing away from him. *"Then why did we run away, why did we lie to those officers?"* She signed. Aiden sighed again, running his hand through his hair. "Because I don't trust the system to be fair. We don't have any physical proof that he killed his gran, or that he planned to kill you. It'll be just hear-say. We need proof if you're going to give yourself in." He said, "we didn't record his

confession so...no proof that he was a psycho either." He shrugged and Isabelle's shoulders sagged. *"So, what do we do now?"* She asked, and Aiden left out a breath he didn't know he'd been holding, relieved. "We need to burn the evidence, we need to act like normal, I'll get us some train tickets home, but in the meantime, we need to act like normal tourists, go some sightseeing, some shopping, then we'll see if were being followed." Aiden said and Isabelle gave him a curious look, *"how come you know all this?"* She asked and he grinned sheepishly at her "spy movies, and I watch a lot of forensic series, I like CSI." He shrugged, "gotta hand it to them, they give good tips." and Isabelle couldn't hold back the smile, he was such a dork. But he was <u>her</u> dork.

He stood, picked up his rucksack and went into the bathroom to get the spoiled clothes. Hesitating he pulled out the old spell book. At the sight of it Isabelle shuddered, *"why do you still have that thing?"* she demanded, a rush of anger filled her at the thought of Cam and what that book held, he gave her a sheepish look, "I...I wanted to look, I needed to know...aren't you curious to what he found out? I mean...we came all this way; can we at least have a look? Surely it wouldn't hurt to look..." Aiden stumbled over the words, he blushed feeling embarrassed. She sighed, she guessed he was right, it couldn't hurt them to look. Plus, she needed to find out what he had said was true, about the cure. She nodded and Aiden sighed with relief, he bought the book over to the bed and sat down. They stared at the little book in his hands, the cover worn and dirty. There was a smudge of dried blood on it, soaked into the top corner on the pages, but it looked much, much older than a night's worth. This must have been from his grandmother. Cam hadn't really let them take a proper look. It was leather bound, with a silver pentagram and silver lettering, something in Romanian no doubt. Aiden and Isabelle took a breath and opened it. A couple of loose sheets fell out, notes from Cam. Aiden picked them up and shook them out. He had neat slanted writing, though it looked rushed. The first sheet read:

*A spell to immobilize:*

*Apa, pământ, foc, aer,*

*Acest spațiu nu îl vom mai împărtăși,*

*Ochi care nu se vor mai vedea,*

*Spiritul care nu mai este liber,*

*Ia de la tine acea lumină interioară,*

*Luați-vă simțurile, sunetul și vederea.*

He wrote the translation in English, besides the incantation.

*Water, earth, fire, air,*

*This space we shall no longer share,*

*Eyes that shall no longer see,*

*Spirit that's no longer free,*

*Take from you that inner light,*

*Take your senses, sound, and sight.*

This must have been what he had used in the tunnels, the strange gust of air that stopped them in their tracks. It listed a bunch of herbs including sage and salt. They turned over the page. There were spells for wealth, spells for good luck, and protection. Until the last page revealed the cure. _Isabelle's cure_ had been handwritten over the top of the page and underlined there several times. Underneath was a different, older handwriting in Romanian, which read like:

*Cu această ofertă,*

*deci, să fie,*

*încheie blestemul care mă suferă,*

*Legati-le de a lor ceea ce este legat de mine,*

*Lasă linia familiei mele să fie liberă.*

*Să se anuleze ceea ce a fost făcut,*

*înainte ca viața mea să dispară.*

*așa că în această noapte Oh, zeiță mă rog,*

*ca să deschizi gura, ca să pot vorbi din nou,*

*ajută-mă să pun capăt acestei suferințe,*

*înainte de a se pierde orice speranță,*

*vă rog să luați oferta mea.*

The English translation for this spell written in Cam's familiar scrawl was penned in underneath.

*With this offering,*

*So, mote it be,*

*End this curse that's suffering me,*

*Bind to theirs what is bound to me,*

*Let my family line be free.*

*Let what was done be undone,*

*before my life is gone.*

*So, on this night, Oh goddess I pray,*

  *that you open my mouth so I may speak again,*

*Help me to end this suffering,*

*before all hope is lost,*

*Please take my offering.*

Underneath the incantation was a list of herbs they would have needed. The spell looked so complex it made Isabelle's head hurt. He had written instructions underneath that made their stomachs churn. The intended victim should already be dead, by the hand of the one who is cursed. Draw a pentagram in your own blood on the victim's chest. Then cut out his/her tongue, place the tongue in a bowl, with the herbs, and burn it at the full moon.

Then once the tongue has burned to ash, mix it with oil and draw a crescent moon on the cursed throat before saying the incantation. The cursed has to shower and sleep when she/he wakes the curse will be lifted. Isabelle shook her head at it. How could Cam think she could do something like this to him? Aiden reached over and took it from her. "Don't..." he said "don't torture yourself over it." She looked up at his face, he looked tired like he hadn't been sleeping very well. With the deep circles under his eyes, he looked older than he had before. *"I'm sorry you got dragged into this...if you want to break up, I understand."* She signed to him, feeling her dark cloud of emotions deepen with sadness and guilt.

"Izzy..." he sighed, kneeling down in front of her. "I don't want to break up with you. Why would you say that?" He asked, tilting her chin up so she would look at him. *"Because, if it wasn't for me, you wouldn't be in this mess..."* she signed *"you would be home, safe."* Aiden shook his head at her "maybe so...but then I'd be alone. I love you, Isabelle, nothing will stop that. This isn't your fault, it's his." He said the last bit darkly, thinking about that arrogance son of a B! made him so angry. *"You mean it?"* She asked, she must have looked insecure because Aiden came over to wrap his arms around her, "I love you, Izzy. I'm going nowhere. Nothing will ever stop me from loving you." he said and as tears pooled in her eyes, she hugged him back.

## CHAPTER 13. ALWAYS DADDY'S GIRL.

The next day Aiden woke Isabelle, gently shaking her shoulder. "Izzy?" He said, "we need to get going," his voice was urgent, which made Isabelle sit up and try to blink away the sleepiness from her. "I booked the train tickets. You need to go shower and get ready, I'm going to get rid of that-" he nodded towards the bin bag. "I'll fetch us some breakfast on the way, be ready for nine o'clock," he said, she frowned but became still as memories from the night before came back to her. The cemetery. Cam. The knife...tears pooled in her eyes and Aiden's face softened. "It'll all be ok, I promise." He said, reaching up to cup her face. He kissed her briefly on the lips but that was all he had time for. They had to get away from this place before anything else could happen.

They had taken the next train out, packing quickly so they could get as far away as soon as possible. Isabelle felt as if the weight of the whole world was pressing down upon her. She had failed, she couldn't save her father, she had failed her mother. Her actions had resulted in the death of not one but two people, even if Cam was crazy. She was a murderer. It took everything in her not to just sit and cry. She could tell Aiden was worried about her, as he kept stealing glances at her and rubbed soothing circles on the back of her hand with his thumb, but what could she do to reassure him when her heart was breaking? She felt a tremendous amount of guilt for bringing him into this and yet here he was, holding her hand and trying to make her feel better, she really didn't deserve him at all. "Wanna go unpack or go straight to the hospital?" Aiden asked as he took out his phone to dial a taxi. *"Hospital, please."* She signed, glad for once in her life that she didn't have to talk. He nodded and relayed the destination to the taxi service before putting the phone down.

He looked over at her and leaned down to place a kiss on her forehead. "Is it ok if I call my parents?" He asked her and she nodded. He brought up the number and pressed dial, pressing it to his ear. "Hi mum..." Aiden said, Isabelle could only just hear, but the relief of his mother and the anger of his father over the other side of the phone made Isabelle feel even more guilty, they had lost a child and no doubt were feeling as if they were going to lose the other. "...How could you do this to us...so worried...school grades..." Aiden's shoulders slumped forwards, he looked tired and ashamed. "I'm sorry...there was something I had to do. Yeah, I'm coming home. Sorry." He talked for a little while longer then ended the call with a sigh. Isabelle tapped him on the shoulder. *"I'm sorry,"* she signed. He gave her a brave smile and said "its fine. I knew I'd be in trouble, but we had to try to save your father." He said it kindly, but it was there in his eyes, it was all for nothing. Tears threatened Isabelle and she began to shake. "Come here," Aiden said pulling her into his arms. In the confines of his arms her pain lessened, with her arms and head tucked up against his chest she felt safe despite everything that had happened.

"It's a mess..." Aiden began "but we still have each other. If Cam had...if you were...I'd have never forgiven myself." He said, she shuddered as she thought of that knife, pictured Aiden's lifeless body on the ground instead of Cam...Aiden's eyes staring at her, glassy and cold. She was suddenly grateful that things had ended the way they did instead of any alternative. "Taxis here, I'll drop you off at the hospital, but I've got to go home, mum and dad...they're not happy with my explanation and I've got to sort things out." Aiden said as he opened the door for her. She nodded at him and got into the car. She would have a lot of making up to do of her own, but she didn't think it would be half as bad as Aiden's would be. Her mother knew why she had to run away, Aiden's family did not. On the way to the hospital she wondered what Aiden planned to tell them.

\*\*\*\*

The hospital was the same it always was, noisy and busy. Her father was still in the same room as he was previously which was good considering Isabelle wasn't the best with directions. She stood outside the room for a moment watching the scene in front of her. Her mother sat on a chair pulled up by her fathers' bed, she held one of his hands in the both of hers. She was hunched slightly and looked as if she were praying. Isabelle examined her mother's face, she looked tired and older somehow. As if she had aged over the few weeks, there was grey at her temples and bags under her eyes...how much of it was Isabelle's doing? She couldn't bring herself to look at her father's face, to see how much he had declined since she saw him last. But she couldn't hold it off much longer.

She hesitated before walking in, the movement drawing her mother's eye. Trish looked up from her husband and her eyes went round. "Isabelle?" She asked her voice trembling. "Is it you! Is it really you?" Her mother darted up from her seat and wrapped her arms around her daughter. "Oh my baby! Let me see you." She said leaning back to loom her over. "Did you...did it work?" She asked, her voice hushed, finally daring to hope, and Isabelle's heart broke at the sight. The tears that threatened to fall when she had stood in the doorway watching them, now fell, running down her face as she shook her head. There was a flash of disappointment in her mother's eyes but she hitched on a brave smile and said. "No matter. I'm still proud of you. At least you tried..." she said, guiding her into the room. Once they were settled she looked her mother over. *"You look tired."* She signed to her. "Oh," her mother reached up to pat her hair own messy, she giggled. "I've not really left the hospital, I was frightened that...he would go when I was away and he would be alone." She said. *"Why don't you get some coffee?"* Isabelle signed *"it might make you feel better, then we can talk."* Her mother gave her a peculiar look, "you're right honey. When did you get so old?" She asked, "you're all grown up." Isabelle just smiled a sad smile at her mother. With a kiss on the forehead and a glance at her husband Trish left for the cafeteria.

Isabelle looked down at her father, at the ashy tones of his skin and the veins on his lids. He looked older; he looked a bit like cam had. Dead. "I don't know what to say." She said knowing it was dangerous to talk but wanting to fill the silence. She had been keeping it in for so long that now she was here, looking down at her father, she was unable to keep it in for a moment longer. And it rushed out of her, like a damn had been broke and the words were water. She told him about finding the caravans, finding Lavinia and Cam. About how he had tricked them and his plans to kill her. She told him how he died, by her hand. How she couldn't perform the cure. ".. so you see, I failed you. I'm so sorry, I failed." She said still looking down at the hand she held, unable to say this to his face. A hand reached up to cup her cheek and she gasped in shock. "Daddy!" She exclaimed, reverting back to the old name she called him. Blue eyes met blue eyes as her father looked up at her. "You didn't fail me, baby girl. You did everything you could and I couldn't be more proud of you." He said his voice weak and hoarse from disuse. Isabelle clutched his hand to her face and smiled at him despite her pain. "Where's your mum?" He asked, looking for her. "She went to get some coffee. She'll be back soon." Isabelle told him, he nodded and smiled and asked, "how much does she know?" He gave her a piercing stare.

"Not much, I'm scared to tell her the whole thing." Isabelle admitted, her mother wasn't a strong person and Isabelle was sure the truth would finish her off. "Good." He said, "it's best to keep this between you and Aiden." Isabelle nodded in agreement, the less people who knew the better. "How are you awake?" Isabelle asked, and her father looked at the machines and tubes surrounding him. "I guess the medication and the treatments are keeping me going for now, but it's only a matter of time before-" he began coughing, making the beeping of the monitors rise and the patterns to spike. He reached up for the cup and straw on the dresser next to him. Isabelle's hand reached up first to get to it. "Here," she said holding it out to him and he took a long draft from the straw. "Thank you," he said, relaxing back into the cushions. "What do we do now?" Isabelle asked, she was scared. "Seems to me you got two choices: you can carry on the way things have always been, use sign language, being careful all your life. Or you can go back, when things have died down and perform the cure." He suggested.

"But what good will come of it? It'll be too late for *you*." Isabelle said and her father shook his head at her, "it shouldn't be about saving me. It will free *you*. You're more important to me than anything or anyone in the world, including myself. Promise me that you won't put yourself in any more danger for me...*promise* me." He said sternly, a hard glint in his eye telling her this was none-negotiable. "I promise, daddy." She signed, then wiped the tears off her face, that seemed to be continuously seeping from her eyes. He smiled then, and she knew he believed her.

Just then her mother returned with the coffee. In her surprise she almost dropped it. "Matthew!" She put every emotion she could muster into that one word, and the look they shared was so intimate that Isabelle felt the love and the pain of it. She came around to the other side of the bed and clasped his hand in hers. "If I'd have known you'd be awake I'd have stayed..." she said he reached up to cup his wife's face. "Its fine, Isabelle was with me." He said. She kissed the palm of her husband's hand. "Could you give us a minute?" Her mother asked her. She nodded and left to go sit out in the hall. Without Aiden she felt lost, adrift. She was alone. It was dangerous for her to be alone with her thoughts, they strayed back to that night. No matter what anyone tells her, she will always be haunted by what she has done.

## CHAPTER 14. THE CLOSE.

Aiden hated funerals. He supposed that no-one liked funerals, but he had been to too many in his life. His grandparents, his twin sister, now Isabelle's father...it was so unfair. Even in black, Isabelle was the most beautiful girl he had ever seen. Even with her face blotchy from crying. He kissed the top of her forehead and she turned from her mother to wrap her arms around his waist. Matthew had lasted a week after he and Isabelle got back, then his organs had begun to shut down and he had slipped away. **It wasn't fair.** Isabelle had given her everything to try to save him but it wasn't enough.

The service has been a subdued one, with not many people but he was glad his parents had allowed him to be here for Isabelle. They had been so very angry with him, he was now grounded for as long as he lived there. He wasn't allowed out of the house except school and chores. It was no more than he deserved, disappearing without a word the way he had. All for nothing. Hatred for Cam boiled up again and he felt he could spit fire. Evil, that's what he was! Reeling them in like that only to betray them. He deserved to rot in hell. He looked around at the people who had shown up, weeping women dabbing at their eyes and men with somber faces. He was surprised to see Mr. Phelps the headmaster towards the back of the congregation. He noticed Aiden watching and nodded at him in acknowledgement. He spotted little Mrs. Medley's stout figure, his very nosy neighbor and figured she was in her element here, plenty of things to gossip about no doubt. He shook his head, they probably never even knew Matthew Golden properly, only through Trish which made Aiden sad.

Was that what life was going to be like for Isabelle? The Priest said something, and Trish came forward, she leaned over and threw down a rose. It hit the coffin with a dull thud. This seemed to make Isabelle cry harder, I kissed the top of her head and murmured to her how much I loved her and how she was so brave. The Priest, a portly older man said: "God, our Father, we entrust Matthew Golden into your hands," he lent forwards and took a handful of dirt, scattering it down upon Matthew as he said:

"From dust you came, to dust you shall return. Jesus Christ, is the resurrection and the life," Trish came forwards and took a handful of dirt, she too let it fall from her fingers to below. Aiden helped Isabelle forward so she could take some of the dirt and as she let it go she mouthed "I'm sorry." A few other people stepped forwards, including his parents and scattered their dirt, paying their respects to a man they never truly knew.

The Priest held up his hands and spoke "Lord God, our Father in heaven, Lord God, the Son, and Saviour of the world, Lord God, the Holy Spirit, have mercy on us. At the moment of death, and on the last day, save us, merciful and gracious Lord God. Let us pray: Our Father in heaven, we thank you that, through Jesus Christ, you have given us the gift of eternal life. Keep us firm in the faith, that nothing can separate us from your love. When we lose someone who is dear to us, help us to receive your comfort and to share it with one another. We thank you for what you have given us through Matthew. We now entrust ourselves to you, just as we are, with our sense of loss and of guilt, When the time has come, let us depart in peace, and see you face to face, for you are the God of our salvation; Amen."

There was a chorus of Amen's as the funeral drew to a close. A dark figure further away drew Aiden's eye. He was standing in the shadows, a familiar shape, a cocky grin, a flash of green. Aiden blinked and the figure was gone. He shook his head. He must be seeing things, it had all been playing on his mind lately, he wasn't sleeping properly-that was it. But he couldn't stop his eyes from being drawn to the same spot, from looking over again, to see if he could see him again. He couldn't shake off the feeling of being **watched**. Isabelle sobbed and clutched at him tighter. "Receive the Lord's blessing. The Lord bless you and watch over you. The Lord make his face shine upon you and be gracious to you. May the Lord look kindly on you and give you peace; In the Name of the Father, and of the Son and of the Holy Spirit. Amen." The priest finished the speech, and everyone murmured their last Amen. As everyone began to filter away, some staying to chat, his parents came over. It was hard seeing the pain and loss on their faces, for surely, they were thinking about Sarah just as he had been. His father patted him on his shoulder.

"Are you staying for the wake?" Trish asked, placing a gentle hand on his shoulder, and smiling bravely. Aiden looked up to his father, who gave a small nod. Things had been rocky between them, but he was gaining their trust again, he felt a moment of gratefulness for them. He had known a normal, happy childhood thanks to them and he could only assume how tough it must have been for Izzy and her family

. "Yeah, we are." Aiden replied to Trish, She smiled and then wrapped an arm around Isabelle; she was a strong woman and despite what had happened she still had Isabelle's back. "Come on honey, we can see Aiden soon, the cars going." She said and Isabelle let herself be led away, leaning on her mother as much as she had lent on him. He loved her very much, and there was no way he was going to let her be hurt, ever again. As he stood there, he vowed to do everything in his power to help her. He would always take care of her, no matter what.

## FOUR YEARS LATER...

The sounds of the thunk of metal on soil, followed by the soft plop of the soil being tossed down was the only sound to be heard in the cemetery that night. Aiden swiped sweat from his brow the only outward sign showing his tiredness. "How much further do you think they buried him?" A voice shouted down. Considering that they had already dug down 3 foot, Aiden replied "At least 4 feet more." He wiped at the sweat beading on his brow with the back of his hand smearing dirt across his forehead. "We're so lucky we found a good hiding place," Kyle said bending over the side of the hole they had begun to dig. "You're lucky he decided not to be cremated." Ollie muttered under his breath as he pushed down on his own shovel, breaking apart the hard earth. Aiden's lips quirked up into an almost smile. "Any Idea how we're going to get out of here after?" Kyle continued looking worried, his usual blasé attitude gone. "I dunno, Climb the fence?" Liam suggested, taking a breather from digging. "Aw man, I hope we don't get caught," Kaiden said he looked scared, his face pale in the moonlight. Aiden was incredibly lucky that when he told the lads what had really happened when he and

Isabelle had 'run away' he was so lucky that they not only believed him they had offered to help. He wasn't so sure they were going to be ok with what had happened, but Izzy's life was at stake, and the baby's...he figured he would take his chances, luckily it paid off. So here they all were, helping him dig up a grave.

Isabelle didn't know about this, she just thought he was out for the night on a drinking spree celebrating their recent graduation, but instead they were here on an illicit bit of grave robbing. "You sure this is going to even work?" Nathan asked, he was the third helping them digging up the grave, along with Liam. Ben, Kyle and kaiden were the look outs. "Yeah, I mean, it's been four years wont he be all...I dunno. There can't be much left of the guy, can there?" Liam asked. Throwing dirt over his shoulder. "Hey!" Kyle shouted down angrily, jumping out of the way of the dirt that Liam threw up. "Sorry," Liam shouted back, as the other two snickered.

"Sssh!!" Aiden hissed "you're making too much noise, someone will hear us!" They glanced around sheepish, worried he was right and that someone would come running over to stop them. "It's worth a shot," Ollie said "in any case, we can just burn the whole body, can't we? Or whatever." Sticking his shovel in, there came a loud thunk! They had hit something. "Come on, help me uncover it," Aiden said. They scrambled to remove the last buy of dirt to reveal the rotting wood of the casket. "Here it is boys." Liam said, "who's going to open it?" Ben asked, in a hushed voice. Now the time had come they were a bit reluctant. It was probably going to smell, a lot. "I'll do it." Aiden said his jaw set. After all it was his decision. He reached down the side of the opening with his shovel and pried it open. The nails were so strong that Ollie, Nathan, and Liam had to use their shovels as well to get it to open, it splintered.

"Stand back," Aiden said and as the others shuffled backwards, Aiden pushed the lid open their eyes half closed in dread of seeing the shriveled corpse of Camilo Bosswell. But the coffin was empty. "What the!" Ben exclaimed, they all leaned over to stare confused at what they had discovered. "But why is it empty?" Kyle asked, "has someone else got here before us?" Ben asked. "Grave robbers?" Ollie suggested. Aiden remained silent, thoughtful. Of course, he thought as he spotted something. "It's not empty," Aiden said, reaching down and snagging a yellowed envelope that was sticking out from under the silk pillow. There was a boyish scrawl in the front that said: Aiden and Izzy. He flipped over the envelope and tore into it pulling out a thick notelet. There was just one line on it but it confirmed his suspicions.

*Did you really think it was that easy? Come find me.*

"Dude! He's *alive?*" Ben said as they all read over his shoulder. They looked at it as if it were an old treasure map, something held with a certain reverence and an excitement for adventure, but Aiden viewed it for what it really was...a dangerous game. With a grim expression he tucked it into his pocket. "What do we do now?" Ollie asked him, "*we* don't do anything," Aiden said "I've already asked enough of you all, I can't drag you into this any further. This guy...he's dangerous." The guys scoffed and shook their heads.

"Do you really think we would let you face this guy alone? If he's as dangerous as you say, then you'll need all the help you can get." Ollie said, a hand on Aiden's shoulder. "Yeah, what kind of a friend would we be if you went up against this guy alone?" Nathan agreed, reaching over to pat his shoulder. "You need us bro," Liam said, also laying his hand on Aiden, "we've got your back," Kyle said rather uncharacteristically, while shy Kaiden said a quiet "We all want to help," looking around at all his friends he felt a warmth in his chest. After the death of his sister, he had never thought that he would ever find a home again. Until now. Until Isabelle. He felt that he could not refuse them.

Seeing his resolve cave in, his friends took a moment to cheer and punch the air. "If it becomes too dangerous, we stop looking." Aiden said, "but if we do find him. You do realize what has to happen." He looked them each in the eye, what he was asking of them...it was too much. It was murder. "We might never find him..." Ollie said, "but if we do-" Aiden began. "We'll deal with it. Until then, we just look for him." Nathan said. "Yeah, and it's all for Izzy, isn't it? And the baby," said Liam said. Aiden sighed, thinking about his family strengthened his resolve. "For Izzy, I'll do anything." He said. The baby wasn't planned, wasn't even *born* yet but his love for it was huge. He loved them both so much he was willing to do what was needed. Ben rubbed his hands together gleefully, looking younger than he was in the moment making Aiden smile. "Well then, let the hunt begin."

R. G. INSKIP

## ABOUT THE AUTHOR

### GET TO KNOW ME BETTER....

My name is Rebecca Georgina Inskip, I live in Newcastle-under-Lyme. In Staffordshire. I was born on the 13$^{th}$ of January 1995. Writing has always been a passion of mine, ever since I was a child, and I've always wanted to be a published Author ever since I learned to pick up a pen. I'd say my inspiration was definitely J.K. Rowling, along with many others, including the likes of Holly Black, Stephenie Meyer and so on.

For me, writing has been so important because I was always told that I could never be a writer, because I have Dyscalculia. Because I have Dyscalculia there's always been a struggle for me to fit in anywhere, I've had several incidences of people calling me 'stupid' or 'thick'. Teachers and College lecturers have constantly put me down, telling me I'm too stupid to be an Author. When I came up with really good course work I was given it back, telling me to 'put it into my own words' and not to just 'copy and paste from the internet' even though these were my own words.

When you have a learning disability people usually just see that and not the potential you have in you. I want to help get rid of this stigma, so people like me have a chance and are not just brushed aside or labelled the way I have been. (for the full story please look on my story on the Amazon Authors page.)

R. G. INSKIP

# THANK YOU FOR READING!

If you have any questions or just want to express your feelings please leave a positive comment on Kindle and Amazon in the feedback section. If you would like to follow me and my progress, see sneak peek previews of new books and photographs go to:

https://www.facebook.com/R.G.Inskip

You can also find me on:

Twitter:

@R_G_Inskip

INSTAGRAM:

@Becca_Inskip

SILENCE IS GOLDEN

Check out some of the authors other books: The Longhorn Academy Trilogy.

*Chosen* is fantasy fiction at its absolute finest and marks the beginning of an exciting and highly addictive fantasy trilogy. When a group of teenagers are invited to join Longhorn Academy - a Scottish monster-hunting school dedicated to teaching the arts of defense and mythology, and combat evil – to become the next generation of Protectors, none are prepared for the precarious and unpredictable adventures which lie ahead. Anything can (and frequently does) happen at this unique school but luckily, each of these teenagers has been bestowed with their own special gift to help them win the epic battle between good and evil. Garnet, Michael, Dani, and Katie are all feisty, memorable, and independent personalities, but when they come together, no one stands a chance against them. And when James, the vampire, ends up living with them in their apartment, the excitement becomes almost palpable. But their strength loyalty and friendships are tested to the Max. Cue every fantasy addicts dream – plenty of magic, a gaggle of werewolves, vampires, protectors, keepers, spells, wizards, mysterious iron keys, a spooked horse, strange cats, and wolves - combined with an utterly compelling love story, dangerous hangovers from past generations and family bloodlines, and you have all the makings of a best-selling fantasy book. One word of warning, however, you must be prepared to devour the book in a single setting because once you start you won't be able to stop reading.

# SILENCE IS GOLDEN

*Underworld* is the second book in the Longhorn Academy Trilogy takes the group to a new level of Danger and Adventure. Longhorn Academy School is a place -set deep in the south west of Scotland-dedicated teaching the Arts of Defense and Mythology and combat Evil-to become the next generation of Protectors. Back from Christmas break, the group have a job to do. Garnet, Michael, Katie, Dani, and James have been training long and hard but now is the time! To free the Vampire James of his affliction they have to journey to the Underworld. Filled with dangerous creatures and deadly seasons they have their work cut out for them, their only hope comes in the form of a brash old Irishman called Smithy, an old acquaintance of James, who has lived in the Underworld for years. The Underworld has many answers about their ancestors past giving them prophetic dreams that are both eye-opening and bewildering. With their gifts growing stronger they have a lot of growing up to do before the year is out. Creepy looking Protector Kyle also has his own problems involving the Fairies and the Vampire Xavier. This book is number two in a series of three that follow a group of teenagers and a Vampire in a dangerous and daring tale of love, friendship and loyalty that will take them to a new level of suspense and thrilling action in this exciting tale, of Vampires, Protectors, magic, talking cats, fairy kingdoms, stone archways, dark caves, smelly bogs, a creepy ferryman and murderous mythological creatures. Highly addictive, once you start reading this book you won't be able to put it down.

Longhorn Academy is a School is a place -set deep in the south west of Scotland-dedicated teaching the Arts of Defence and Mythology and combat Evil-to become the next generation of Protectors. The group are back again in this last tale of the trilogy, *Prophecy.* Join Michael, Garnet, Katie, Dani, and James after they have finished their mission in the Underworld as it is now it's time to face the consequences of their actions. With Xavier holding Protector Kyle's sister hostage the group must call their allies to arms. They have to gather their own magical army together if they are to defeat Xavier and his legion, but will it all be enough to stop him? Michael, Garnet, Katie, and Dani have only just scratched the surface of their powers and it is now time for them to harness their gifts and use them to help win this war. But death is inevitable, Garnet has a big choice to make-a sacrifice, ensuring it will all end in bloodshed and heartache. A word of warning however, once you start reading you must be prepared to devour the book in a single setting because you won't be able to stop reading.

*All three books are available in*

*Kindle and Book form on*
*Amazon.com and on Kindle bookstores.*

Printed in Great Britain
by Amazon